Lustful

Intentions

Annaca Reybella Chronicles

K. B. Rebel, Kat Jackson

Lazy Witch Crafts Publications

<u>Introduction</u>

Mature Adult Content

This Is Your Only Warning

Lustful Intentions

A woman of 25 chasing after her happily horny after, Weston (30), while meeting Mr. & Mrs. Right Now along the way. Annaca Amber Reybella has a craving that remains unsatisfied despite her many attempts. She followed a man with lustful intent, but she enjoys sampling the menu while she waits for her main course. Dabbling in different kinks, she tries to scratch that temptress of an itch that taunts her day and night.

In this adventure... Annaca's desire for psychical touch has taken over her capability to think straight. Man or Woman. It doesn't matter when she is on the hunt for a playmate. A gorgeous farmhand walks into her marketing agency looking for representation as she mentally ravishes him in sinful ways. Her adrenaline kicks up a notch with the thrill of getting caught in the act.

I wrote this book before trigger warnings existed, so I am not putting in the warnings because that ruins the book!

Chapter One

Wet Dreams

She let out a deep sigh as he grabbed the back of her head and pulled her into a kiss. His lips were warm and soft, like the velvet of a rose petal. It was a simple kiss, but it felt like electricity going through her entire body. Reluctantly, he pulled away from her lips as she opened her eyes and gazed into his startling green eyes. *His eyes are like sparkling emeralds*, she thought.

He leaned in to kiss her again, and she was eager to comply, ready with a deep hunger for his kiss. She slowly placed her hands around his jaw, framing his face to pull him as close as she could. As they kissed, he caressed her with deft strokes. Her heart fluttered with excitement as she pleaded in her mind, *please don't let this end.*

She could feel his hands slide slowly toward her hips and down to the outer sides of her thighs. With a shocking suddenness, he hoisted her up and pressed her into the brick wall. She wrapped her legs around his waist and crushed her mouth to his. Trailing her fingertips from his face to his bulging arms, she could feel the tenseness of his muscles.

Her long ebony hair interrupted their kissing as it floated in the breeze, falling between their lips. She silently begged for him to take her to the next level, she wanted more than kissing. Gently, she traced his body with wandering fingertips around his shoulders down to the small of his back. Hesitantly, she grazed his hips with her fingertips and moved to his cold silver belt buckle. He gently kissed her neck, encouraging her to proceed.

Both were so fixated on the other, there was no concern for their, oh so very, public location. He teasingly caressed her thigh and slid his hand up under her filmy skirt on her leg toward her right hip, admiring the smoothness of her skin underneath his questing fingers. He playfully tugged on her white lace panties. Her heart was racing with the idea that she would get what she wanted tonight.

She couldn't take it anymore. She wrenched his buckle open and snatched his belt from the loops around his waist. She held his belt out and teasingly shook it. He looked at her with intensity that sparked a molten ache deep in her core, then grinned as she dropped his belt and her hands went for his zipper. He leaned in and gently blew on her neck. His tongue grazed her neck as he lightly started sucking at the sensitive crook of her neck, sending shivers through her body.

She dropped his pants, reached further down to determine what he had to offer her. His substantial length was rock hard, showing her that he was wanting her just as much as she wanted him. She needed to feel him deep inside of her. She hungered to feel his fingers stroking her wetness, pleasing her. Bracing her with his right arm and body, he pressed her against the brick wall and slid her panties to the side so he could rub her clit with his first two fingers. The warmth of his touch had her so close to climax.

Thud! Just like that, Annaca woke up with a dull ache in her ass. She had fallen out of bed again. All hot and sweaty, she was even hornier than usual after a dream like that. Desperately, Annaca desired to find a talented man who could indulge all of her fantasies. Regular sex wasn't going to satisfy her appetite for that rough edge of passion and a touch of pain. She desired that physical touch you only read about in books or seen in movies. She craved to be embraced with the heat from another's body.

Imagining the man in her dreams to be six foot tall with those gorgeous emerald eyes, jet black hair, and muscles rippling across his whole body like the waves of the ocean. His expressive face was a chiseled in stone masterpiece. He had a smile that could out shine the full moon. He was an Adonis, perfection of her mind's design.

A dream, it was just that, her imagination running wild, looking for mind blowing sex that she had not yet experienced. The possibility seemed elusive when it came to a physical relationship that required a partner. Just the heat of a human touch and it could send her body into a submission of ecstasy.

The sun glistened through the window onto her rumpled scarlet satin bed cover. The queen sized bed was soaked with sweat from her midnight fantasy. Another dream ruined, leaving Annaca with a thirst for more. It had to be at least seven A. M. but her alarm didn't go off, maybe she could get another hour of sleep and pick up where she left off.

She reached for her phone that was on her bed side table. Sleep still in her eyes, she checked the time... eight o'clock.

"Oh hell, I'm late!" She exclaimed aloud.

With a deep sigh, she shifted her legs to the side of her bed and slid her feet onto the cool wooden floor. She glanced into her dresser mirror and saw she had eyeliner streaking her face from tossing and turning.

Rubbing her eyes to wipe away the streaks, she continued to the kitchen to get a cup of her favorite brew, Colombian dark roast with a splash of Italian sweet creamer. Slowly, she sipped her coffee to soothe her dry, irritated throat. She only had a moment or two since she was already late, as always.

Swiftly, she went to her closet and threw open the doors. Bits of her dream flashed in her mind as she scrambled through her dresser and closet to find her outfit for the meeting. She had her clothes and accessories tossed onto her chaise lounge. An ivory button down blouse with a gray flowing skirt with basic black pump heels to keep it business-like attire.

A thin silver chain draped around her neck, matching the earrings that dangled to her jaw line. Silver Celtic knot flat rings to go on each middle finger. Dressed and ready for her work day, out the door she headed downtown, hopping onto the city bus and rode to her firm, which was a few miles away.

Even though she didn't know it, today, her dream was about to become a mysterious reality. The touch she craves would soon happen. The tall, dark, and handsome man that taunts her playful inner demons was just around the corner. He would be perfection in physical form. He would help to ease her pent up sexual tension that has been haunting her in her dreams.

Chapter Two

Business First

Although she did not know it at that moment, her new client was going to kick off a sexual journey that she only dreamed about. Annaca was young, but that didn't stop her hormones from building up. She was a strong, outgoing girl who was ready to take on the world one client at a time.

Annaca worked downtown at Acker & Hill Advertising. They are well known for their work. Their own advertisements are seen everywhere, including city buses to enormous billboards lining the interstate. She has worked for going on five years building advertising packages for their clients. She created starter kits to launch the client's business off the ground.

Being one of the youngest to climb their corporate ladder, she was always watched for any actions, good or otherwise. Twenty-three and she had already outsold the entire firm. She was not only hated for her appearance but she was despised by coworkers for her ability to sell. All she had to do was flash that blinding smile and bat her long, dark eyelashes, and clients were sold.

Her coworkers would do anything to sabotage her and ruin her status in the firm. They were petty women who had lost their youth to the stress of life. Instead of finding a new career, the petty flourished in the ideas of desperation and deceit. The drama never ends at high school; it continues through the rest of life. Annaca wasn't concerned with the petty pea-bodies of the office though. She knew that her work was efficient.

Weston approached the shimmering glass doors of Acker & Hill advertising. As he opened the door and glanced to the right, gold lettering on the wall sign, gave direction to his destination. Weston stood six foot three with a panty dropping grin and mesmerizing emerald eyes. His hair was dark as a moonless sky.

He possessed a body that was gym model quality with a bronzed, muscular build. Although in a business suit, his country upbringing still shone through in his mannerisms. Weston's callused hands gripped a black leather briefcase.

Weston breezed through the meeting room doors as Annaca looked up to greet her new client. *Whoa*! She thought as her mind shifted to her dream of the night before. *Am I still asleep? How can this be possible? H*er imagination took off, and she quivered with images of Weston laying her down on the glass table in front of everyone.

He was tearing her skirt off as she ripped his white button down shirt wide open to reveal his chiseled chest. His velvet kiss was teasing her neck, and his hands venturing to new territories of her body. She grinned as she pulled him on top of her and gripped his firm ass. He was about to remove her panties when a deep voice interrupted.

"Excuse me, Ma'am, am I in the right meetin' room?" A southern drawl snapped her back to the room as she charmingly smiled at him.

"Yes, I'm sorry you caught me off guard, you're in the correct room." Annaca answered.

This was him, the man of her fantasies. It was as if she had pulled him from her dream and into the office. Weston was Annaca's dream in a three piece business suit standing in front of her waiting to hear her sales pitch.

"You don't look like an inventor; you look like a model out of a magazine." Annaca blurted out loud.

Annaca froze as she realized she had just blurted that out in front of the staff. The petty pea-bodies already took note that she was being flirtatious with Weston and were whispering to each other about her shamelessly scandalous behavior.

Annaca paused and said, "I'm so sorry. I didn't mean to say that. That was unprofessional and rude, I apologize again."

Weston chuckled and said, "Thank you, ma'am, I'll take that as a compliment."

Annaca blushed with a wave of embarrassment, "Shall we get started?"

Weston was amused by Annaca's blushing cheeks, "Yes ma'am, we shall indeed."

Annaca drew a deep breath and started to speak, "From your designs, I can tell that your product will sell itself. I'm not sure that we can really help you."

Weston's smile faded as he spoke, "I design nylon ropes to further assist the climbers, campers, and hunters. These ropes have many uses, and I can show you with a small demonstration. They can be used in every household. Need to tie something up? There's a rope for it. Need to move a large object or furniture and keep your tarp in place? There's a rope for that as well."

He paused for a moment.

Weston finished by explaining, "I work with farm equipment most days, and the idea just came to me as I snapped a rope one day. Ropes can have many uses, but they need to have strength."

Intrigued yet unable to help much, Annaca said regretfully, "I'm truly sorry, but I don't see where our firm can help you. What I can do is put together a small business kit to present to a financial institute if you are looking for funding."

With a grimace of disappointment, Weston started to pack up his briefcase to exit the office.

"Thank you for your time, ma'am. I appreciate the offer. Maybe I can work with that for starters. Here's my card, will you mail that packet to this address?" He asked with a smoldering look.

"I would be happy to help in any way that I can," Annaca replied.

Weston gave a little salute and headed out the door.

Annaca paused for a moment as she glanced around the office. Her curiosity urged her to follow Weston to the main entrance.

"Sir, please wait, could I talk to you for a moment?" Annaca requested. *I can't believe I am doing this*, she thought.

Weston stopped and spun around to look at who called out. As he turned, he was so close to Annaca they could have kissed right there in the lobby.

"Pardon me, Ma'am," exclaimed Weston. "How can I help you?"

Annaca blushed again and wanted to embrace his lips with hers and fulfill her fantasy right there in the lobby.

Stuttering a bit, she asked, "Weston, was it? Listen, I'm not usually this bold, but I have to ask if you would meet me for dinner tonight? I may be able to personally help you with your products and see if we can find a proper way to approach a sales technique."

Nonplussed, Weston replied, "I don't know about that, ma'am. I'm not quite sure. You said that it doesn't seem like you can help me with my business."

Tentatively, Annaca replied, "Well how about dinner at Makko's to discuss that? I'm sure I can help you somehow. It's my pleasure, I mean, my treat. I would really like to help you in any way I can."

Weston sighed and said, "Well, ma'am, I would feel downright awful if I let you pay for dinner. How about 7 pm at Makko's and we don't discuss business?"

Butterflies fluttered in her stomach as she grinned and then nodded as she accepted his dinner proposal. "Sounds wonderful, I shall see you then."

Weston smiled and then turned back to the glass doors, where he exited with a twinkling of pleasure in his eyes.

Annaca was overwhelmed with hormonal reactions and could not wait until her dinner appointment with her Adonis.

It was five o'clock, and Annaca rushed home to prep for this dinner. Visions of him pinning her to the satin blanket that covered her bed danced in her mind. *Could this finally be what she desired so much*? She questioned.

She shook her head to clear her thoughts. She was thrilled and couldn't wait to see him again. There was no way she was going to pass up an opportunity to try and take advantage of this southern gem.

Chapter Three

Dinner Date

Annaca stripped out of her business clothing and paraded her naked body to her bathroom. Her bathroom was ivory and black tile with and old style cast iron tub with a porcelain toilet and pedestal sink to match. The vintage light fixtures would flicker. The old wiring was questionable. She lived alone in her one bedroom flat.

The floors were solid wood, with walls that were brick painted an eggshell color. Her flat was above an old movie theater that only opened on weekends to show old movies. Her windows were antique wooden framed, single pane, covered with sheer scarlet drapes to match her bedding. There was an eerie feeling to her flat, but she was comforted by the quiet settling of the building. The water pipes creaked and clanked. The wooden floors groaned as she walked across them. It was her first place when she moved away from home.

She glanced in the mirror like most girls do; looking for flaws that probably were not there and then checking her body to make sure it was perfect for her date. She turned the water on and checked the temperature so it wasn't too hot.

Placing the stopper in the tub, she climbed in and watched the water slowly fill up and caress her body. Leaning back, she swayed her foot back and forth under the faucet water as it trickled down to her hip and pooled beside her.

Reaching for her sponge and her favorite soap, she began to lather her body. Soaking for a moment, she tilted her head back and imagined Weston walking through her bathroom door and offering to assist. She grazed her own body with the tips of her fingers as if they were his. Slowly and teasingly touching each part of her body and making it quiver with pleasure. His velvet kiss haunted her thoughts.

Her fantasy was interrupted by the sound of her cell phone ringing in the distance. She ducked under the water to rinse off and splashed back up to reach for her towel. She climbed out of her tub, drying her feet on the soft microfiber rug; she wrapped the towel around her body and headed for her phone.

She had a missed call. Her best friend, Carlene, had called. They were supposed to go for drinks that evening. Annaca had completely forgotten about their night out the moment she laid eyes on Weston. She thought about calling her back, but this date was too important to pass up.

So she texted instead.

Annaca: *Hey, I met a guy today, and he is gorgeous in every way. He asked me out on a date tonight, and I can't pass this up. Rain check for tomorrow and I will tell you all about it?*

Carlene: *Alright, well he better take care of your hormones if you are going to ditch me! Lol.*

Annaca: *That is my plan. I'm wearing the black satin halter dress with the slit up the side.*

Carlene: *Oooh girl, no man can resist that dress. Get it! Don't forget to message me when you get home. Love you girl.*

Annaca smiled down at her phone as she responded.

Annaca: *Love you too.*

Thankfully, Makko's was just four blocks away from her flat. Annaca glanced at the time, and it was 6:15pm.

She flinched and realized she had better hurry. She took her towel from around her body, wiped her face and dried her ebony hair. Annaca was fortunate that she never had a bad hair day, so she ran a brush through her hair and tossed the brush onto the bed.

That black satin dress hung in her closet. Because it hugged her form perfectly, it was the best first date dress. She pulled it from her closet and removed the hanger. She slipped her legs through and pulled the halter piece over her head.

Annaca smoothed the dress down with her hands, and she couldn't wait to have his hands all over her body. She was determined to make this dream a reality. She needed this man to ease some of her sexual frustration.

Another check in the mirror, a touch up here and there of her makeup, and she was out the door and headed to Makko's. The excitement in her was boiling over. As she stepped out onto the sidewalk, her shimmering black open-toed heels were clicking with every step she took. Just one more block and she would be in front of Makko's.

She reached the entrance of Makko's within a few minutes. Makko's was a local hangout with a hometown feel for country life. A steak and ale house with a Southern touch. Since it was Friday, the special was sirloin with a choice of potato and a vegetable.

Annaca always got the special, a simple taste that reminded her of home. She wasn't picky about what she ate and she loved her red meat.

Glass double doors with the rounded black handles stood in front of her. Annaca drew a deep breath and pulled on the right door handle and proceeded to walk into the restaurant. Glancing around the room, her eyes darted to each dark haired man, searching for him. *Please say he is* here *somewhere,* she pleaded in her mind. Her heart almost stopped when she saw him.

Weston looked directly at Annaca, and their eyes locked. Annaca smiled as Weston gave her that Southern charm grin and a wave. Annaca calmly walked over to the table where Weston was seated. He slid his chair out and stood up to greet her. Weston eased past her to the other chair and pulled it back with a hand gesture for her to sit.

Annaca accepted gracefully and sat down. As Weston returned to his seat and sat down, his eyes were scanning her body and examining her dress. The front of her dress displayed the tops of her supple breasts to perfection. Annaca knew this was the right dress for tonight. *He can't take his eyes off of me*, she thought.

Just when she assumed this dinner was going to be normal; Weston stood up and cleared the table with one swipe of his muscular arm. He walked over to her seat and offered his hand for her to stand up. Annaca gracefully accepted and stood. Weston placed his strong hands around her waist, picked her up and laid her softly onto the table.

He leaned over and gently started caressing her neck with his lips. He worked his way down to the point of the bust line in her dress. His hands started massaging her thighs, with his finger tips flirting with the hem of her dress. *Yes, right here, right now, I don't care who's watching*, Annaca mentally insisted.

Interrupting Annaca's mini fantasy, Weston asked, "So, what would you recommend to eat here?"

Blushing, she picked up the menu quickly and started glancing over it, Annaca replied, "I find the house sirloin to be of top quality."

Weston raised his right eyebrow and said, "Don't meet many city girls that like steak."

Amused, Annaca replied tartly, "Don't meet many country boys like you in the city. Just because I live in the city doesn't make me a city girl! I was raised in a little country town. Problem is, work can only be found in the city."

Weston smirked at her sassy reply and apologized for his statement. They waved to their server, a young man of maybe twenty-one, to place their order. The playful banter went back and forth all through dinner.

Annaca was hanging on every word that Weston spoke. His voice was deep, and that drawl was charming and alluring. All she could think about was the dream she had the night before, and there he was. Her ideal physical manifestation of pleasure and he sat right in front of her.

The food was delicious as always, and the conversation was worth the bold advance in the lobby of Acker & Hill after the meeting. How lucky could she get to run into her personal fantasy at work? She was on cloud nine.

Weston glanced at his watch and said, "Well, ma'am, I have enjoyed your company and appreciate your time, but I do need to get going. May I walk you to your car?"

Disappointed, Annaca replied, "I don't have a vehicle, but I do live four blocks away from here. Would you like to come back to my place for drinks?"

Weston smiled and said teasingly, "Now what kind of gentleman would I be if I didn't at least walk you home?"

Weston stood up and walked over to Annaca's chair and pulled it out so she could stand up. Grinning with enticement, Annaca stood up and started to gather up her clutch and straighten her dress. As they left Makko's out the glass doors, Weston held the door for Annaca. Sweetly she smiled, walked out and waited for Weston as he held the door for an elderly couple. The couple passed through the doors and thanked him for being so kind.

Chapter Four

Show Time

Upon leaving the restaurant, Weston offered his arm for her to hold as he waited for her to direct the way to her home.

"It's dark, and a lady of your quality should not be walking home alone," said Weston.

Here we go, Annaca thought as she took his arm and pointed down the street toward her flat. As they walked, Annaca explained that she lived above an old theater and that it showed old movies on the weekends.

"Well, that is classic. Maybe we can catch a movie tomorrow evening, while I'm still in town for the week."

"You're only in town for a week?" Annaca asked.

"Yes, ma'am, I'll be heading back to the countryside next Thursday." Weston answered.

Annaca pouted at the thought. "Well, here's my place," she said.

They were standing in front of the old Price Theater. The structure was strong for its age. It was built around the 1920's.

"Would you like to come in for a drink?" Annaca asked.

"I really shouldn't, ma'am. I have some work to finish up at my hotel." replied Weston politely.

"I don't want to beg, but how else am I going to get the chance to know you while you are in town?" Annaca pleaded.

Weston wiped his forehead, sighed and then said, "I shouldn't drink, but I can visit a little while longer, I suppose."

Annaca leaned with her back against the theater and gave a beckoning smile. Weston sheepishly stepped closer.

"So, of all places, why did you choose my firm to meet with?" Annaca asked.

Weston grinned and replied, "No business now. That's for an office."

"I could do a lot in an office, if you let me." Annaca flirted.

Annaca gave a devilish grin and apologized while slowly reaching out to pull him closer to her.

Weston caught her hand with his, smiled and said, "Ma'am, if I didn't know any better, I'd think you're trying to sneak in a kiss."

"Would it be a bad thing if I were?" Annaca teased.

"Well... I don't suppose so," Weston replied shyly.

Annaca reached again for Weston. She gently slipped her finger through the middle button of his pale blue button down shirt, hooked it around his button and pulled for him to lean in for that kiss.

Weston seemed so shy but did as she motioned for. Closing his eyes, he leaned in and gently started to press his lips into hers. Annaca returned the kiss and reached for the back of his head so she could pull him in more. Weston placed his hands on either side of her against the warm brick.

Continuing to kiss her with a hunger, Weston slid his left hand down the wall to her waist to feel the satin of her dress and smoothness of her curves. Now he was the one desiring her. He wanted to ravish her right there up against that warm brick wall. The warmth of the wall had nothing on the heat that Annaca was radiating. Slowly, Weston caressed her body from her hip and up to her side.

Annaca shivered each time his hand grazed her body. His muscles bulged as he held himself with one hand and fondled her with the other. Pressing her into the wall with his kiss, she wanted so much more.

Annaca playfully tugged at Weston's jeans. Slipping her fingers in and out of his belt loops. She occasionally freed a shirt button from its threaded clasp. His chest was firm yet smooth to the touch. Annaca leaned in to kiss his chest and worked her way up to his neck. She could smell his sweet, musky cologne. Weston moaned as she ravaged his neck with her questing lips.

Weston taunted Annaca by running his fingers up and down the inside of her left thigh. His fingertips grazed the edge of her panties and sent a shock through her body. Hungrily, he started kissing her lips as he moved to her neck and down her chest. His hand swept up her body to her supple breasts. Caressing them, he slipped his hand into her top to further expose her creamy white skin. She was soft to the touch and taste.

Massaging her nipple with his tongue, he slid his hand down her body and up under her satin dress. Slipping his hand inside the edge of her lacy panties, his fingertips mapped out a hidden treasure. Annaca moaned with every stroke of Weston's fingertips. He continued massaging her gently by tracing her inside and out until she felt her knees shaking, letting his fingers entice her until she was wet and her juices seeped down his hand.

He pulled his hand up to taste her sweetness coating his fingertips. Softly, he put a finger to her lips, and she licked his finger from the base to the tip. Weston grinned. He pulled his hand away and began gently thrusting his finger into her sweet wetness. Annaca pulled his shirt off to expose his muscular arms and grasped his bare shoulders with her nails.

Slowly, Annaca raked her fingers down Weston's back. When she reached his hips, she swept to the front of his waist to his belt loops. Feeling his cold silver belt buckle in her grasp, she wrenched it apart, exposing the button and zippered entrance to her desire. She relieved him of his button clasp and pulled it to the side as the zipper fell. Annaca put a hand on each hip while slipping her fingers into his boxers.

She slid his boxers and jeans down to show his award-winning V cut. Every inch of this man was built for satisfaction. She reached down to feel a stiff, throbbing tool of pleasure in her hand. She ran her fingers up and down his shaft from the tip to where it met the V cut. She wanted to feel him inside her.

Weston was ready to give her what she was asking for. Shifting his hips upward, he could feel her warmth, and it made him want to thrust up inside her. He didn't want to hurt her, though. Ever so gently, he eased his way into her. He began with mini thrusts at first and worked into full strokes. The moment he was fully inside of her, Annaca let out a moan that could be heard around the block.

She put her hands around his waist and dug her fingers into his hips. She wanted him to thrust harder and faster. The intensity of his thrust was hitting her g-spot, and it had her ready to climax. It was so strong that she felt like she was about to explode. He had her quivering with pleasure. Only a few more strokes and they both would climax into ecstasy.

Both of them were thriving to continue into their desires when they were startled by a couple passing by. They froze in their current position as the couple passed. Weston had a look of embarrassment in his eyes. Annaca wasn't worried at all, but she was trying to reassure him that he wasn't doing anything wrong.

The couple got a few paces away and Weston and Annaca heard the woman exclaim in distance, "Why don't we ever try that?"

Her gentleman looked at her and shrugged his shoulders as he motioned for her to move forward and out of sight. Weston and Annaca shook their heads and gave a nervous little laugh.

Weston had lost his urge to finish, so he pulled out of her and tried to place her on the ground, trying to help her return her dress to its proper position. Shyly, Weston adjusted himself and pulled up his pants. He then fastened his belt. Annaca looked at him and pouted.

"I'm so sorry, we need to stop. I don't want to, but I really must get going," explained Weston.

"We can go up to my flat if you are worried about anyone seeing us," pleaded Annaca.

"It's not that, I, I just have a lot to do tomorrow and I must go. I will call you, and maybe we can catch that movie tomorrow," Weston said.

Annaca stood there against the wall and wondered what happened. They were almost there, and he just quit on her. Weston leaned in and kissed her passionately.

As he pulled out of the kiss he said, "I'm so sorry. I promise I will make it up to you, Darlin'."

Annaca pouted again and said, "I'm going to hold you to that promise."

He grinned at her and replied, "I truly hope that you do."

He kissed her once more and walked her to the bottom entrance of her flat. He waited for her to unlock the door, then he kissed her cheek and turned away to walk back toward Makko's where his truck was parked. Annaca wondered if she would see him again. She shook her head in disappointment and walked up to her flat.

Chapter Five

Three Ways

I t had only been a week since Weston left her standing below her flat, unsatisfied. He promised to call and keep in touch as they always do, but she hadn't heard from him. She didn't want to be a pest, so she didn't message him until today.

Annaca: *Hey there, I was wondering if everything was okay.*

She waited for a response. *No reply. No, fuck you, have a nice life, nothing.*

They didn't even get to finish what they started. She was abandoned just at the height of climax, and she needed a release. Even if it was only the one time, she couldn't get enough. Annaca still had the thirst for pleasure, and she needed more to satisfy it.

Another work week, and she tried to concentrate. She had client files laid out across her faux wooden desk. She glanced out the window occasionally, looking for someone to ease her sexual tension. Sitting at her desk, she was checking over her files, and her thoughts were wandering aimlessly. *Where could she find another strapping man to take her on a pleasure ride?*

Pausing from her thoughts, she looked up as a young woman delivered a package onto her desk.

"I need your signature just here, please." The courier smiled sweetly.

"Thank you," she said as she winked and walked away to her next destination.

Rubbing her temples, Annaca contemplated a female partner. *She is sweet and supple; I wonder what it would be like to touch her?*

Annaca got up from her desk and rushed to the firm's main entrance. Following another stranger to the lobby, Annaca searched for the courier. When she spotted her.

Annaca called out to the courier, "Miss, could I speak to you for a moment?"

"I could help but notice you winked at me. I'm not positive that I am reading the sign right, and I may be embarrassing myself, but I was wondering if you would like to join me for drinks some night," Annaca asked.

Blushing at the question, the courier smiled and nodded.

"Yes, you read my signal correctly. That would be great. I know a place downtown, Makko's, do you know it?" The courier asked.

"Of course, that's my favorite place; it's just down the street from my flat. We could go this evening if you would like." Annaca inquired.

"Sure, that sounds wonderful. I finish my route around six. We can meet up around nine-ish," answered the courier.

She extended a hand to Annaca.

The courier quirked a smile as she said, "By the way, my name is Tessa."

Annaca grinned as she shook her hand.

"Annaca, it's a pleasure to meet you. I will see you this evening."

They smiled at each other and went their separate directions. Annaca returned to her office to finish out her day.

Sitting in her office, Annaca was daydreaming and twirling her pen through her fingers. *It's just drinks, no harm in a drink*, she thought. Annaca was nervous. This was her first attempt with a woman. She thought about how she would start if Tessa was interested.

How would she propose such an act? She thought about it throughout the rest of her day. Her hormones were still inflamed, so her imagination had no problems answering her mental questions.

Five o'clock rolled around, and Annaca rushed out the office with her briefcase in her hand. She walked down to the corner where she caught the local bus that ran right by her flat. She wanted to get a head start on her outfit.

When she got to her flat, she stripped down and tossed her work clothes over her armchair. The same chair she would curl up in and read when she wanted to relax. She went through her closet and decided to change into a silk tank top and a flowing black skirt. Before she got too far, she rummaged through her kitchen for a snack. Her stomach was growling, and she couldn't drink on an empty stomach.

Exploring the contents of her fridge, she found some leftover Chinese shrimp and rice. Annaca tossed it into the microwave and grabbed a spoon out of the drawer. She ate quickly because she wanted to be as alluring as she could. She had never tried to see a woman, so she still was unclear on what to do or expect.

After eating, she went to her bathroom to look in the mirror. She freshened up her makeup, and she sprayed on a bit of her favorite scent. The fragrance of baby powder and faint lilacs wafted through the air of her flat. Anytime she went out, her flat would smell like her perfume for a day or two. She deemed her makeup satisfactory and brushed her teeth. She was ready to get to Makko's.

She exited her flat and descended the stairs to the exterior door that led to the outside world. She took a deep breath and exhaled as she closed the second door and locked it. Nervous energy welled up inside of her as she quickly walked to Makko's.

She opened the glass doors and scanned the room. As she looked over by the bar, her eyes locked onto Tessa. Her curly red hair was just above the shoulders. She was still in her work uniform, but she was adorable.

As Annaca walked toward the bar, Tessa's crystal blue eyes called to Annaca. Pausing to take a deep breath, Annaca inhaled with confidence as she made her way through the restaurant.

Tessa was athletically toned with creamy ivory skin to complement her red hair. Annaca could only imagine what she looked like with her clothes off. Her heart fluttered for a moment as a different sensation fueled her desire.

Annaca pulled out the bar stool to the left of Tessa and said, "Hey, I'm so glad we could meet up."

"Me too. I love this place. You can have dinner or just hang out. It's a comfy, yet classy little place. So, what are we drinking tonight?" asked Tessa.

Annaca grinned and replied, "I was thinking sex on the beach. They are delicious and go down smooth."

Tessa nodded in agreement with a saucy grin.

They motioned to the bartender so they could order their drinks. The bartender was a handsome man. He had a muscular physique with deep blue eyes, tan skin that was accented with rich chestnut brown hair. He was eye candy for the customers. His name was Jamie.

It was a quiet night at the establishment. So, the girls had Jamie all to themselves. They chatted the night away and occasionally, Annaca caught Tessa checking her out. Annaca smirked and winked at Tessa the following time she caught her.

It was getting close to closing time, so Annaca wondered if inviting Tessa back to her place would be acceptable.

"Tessa, what do you think about going back to my place after this? I have a full bar at my flat, and it's only four blocks away."

Tipsy and feeling the alcohol set in, Tessa asked, "Can we bring Jamie with us?"

"I don't know, hey Jamie, what do you think, after bar party at my place," asked Annaca.

Jamie was cleaning glasses as he looked up with a grin and said, "sure ladies, let me just finish up here first."

Giggling like schoolgirls, Annaca and Tessa watched Jamie finish up his chores. Jamie closed up and walked the ladies to the door and locked up.

"Are we ready, ladies?" Jamie asked as he offered an arm to each lady.

They both nodded as they accepted an arm while on their way out the door.

Upon reaching the flat, Annaca gave a short history lesson about her beloved theater. She commented on each creaking sound on the old wooden steps as they climbed the stairs to her flat. She opened her flat for her company and pointed out her little bar that sat in the corner. Annaca mixed up drinks for them, and they continued to chitchat.

As they finished their second drink, Tessa had a sly look on her face as she asked, "So, what would you like to do?"

Annaca had been waiting for this moment, so she replied with an eyebrow raise, "Depends... on what you are willing to do."

With a bit of hunger in her eyes, Tessa walked over to Annaca and pushed her down onto her chaise lounge. Jamie watched with an unabashed hunger as Tessa climbed on top of Annaca and began to kiss her. This kiss was different. She tasted sweet, like strawberries and cream.

As Annaca kissed Tessa, she put one hand on her back, slowly caressing her while slipping her hand under her work shirt. With ease, Tessa leaned up, raising her arms so Annaca could remove her shirt to reveal her cute pink lace bra with young supple breasts that Annaca wanted to taste.

Slipping her hand up to the bra snap, Annaca snapped her fingers, and it was off. Tessa smiled as she grasped Annaca's hands and placed them on her perky breasts. Annaca couldn't help but smile; they were perfection in her hands. Annaca played with them while Tessa was kissing her up and down her neck. Tessa was getting aroused, and she started to grind into Annaca's lap.

The more Annaca touched her, the more Tessa would grind her body into Annaca. For this being her first time with a woman, Annaca was overwhelmed with hormonal emotions and was enticed to try other things. Caressing Tessa's body, Annaca's hands ventured toward her pants. Slowly rubbing on her hips and running her hand up and down her zipper.

Annaca unbuttoned Tessa's pants and tugged the zipper down, showing Tessa's matching pink lace panties. Tessa placed both hands on either side of Annaca so she could brace herself up while Annaca removed her pants. Wanting to taste Tessa, Annaca yanked her pants off and then slid her fingers under the sides of her panties to pull them down. Annaca marveled at Tessa's body for a moment.

She just couldn't believe this girl wanted her the way that she does. She pulled Tessa down to kiss her mouth passionately. Annaca wrapped her arms around Tessa, and rolled over so that Tessa was under her. She wanted to take the top and get a taste of Tessa. Their eyes were locked on each other as Annaca gently laid Tessa down on her back.

Tessa grinned up at Annaca and quivered with the idea of what was about to happen. Before Annaca could get one lick in, Tessa grabbed Annaca's head and pulled her back for a kiss. Annaca kissed her and then proceeded to kiss and lick all the way down Tessa's body. Annaca drew a trail with her tongue to the sweet gem that she wanted to indulge in. One flick of Annaca's tongue against her clit and Tessa moaned deeply.

Jamie had hungrily watched all of this from the side, and he wanted in on the fun. As Annaca was pleasuring Tessa, Jamie walked over to the girls and asked if he could join in. He was ready to please. He had two gorgeous girls all to himself. This was the fantasy that most men only dreamed about.

Jamie was a casual friend whom Annaca would take home occasionally. He was able to scratch that itch when Annaca needed it most. She was curious to see if he could handle two girls at once. She loved his witty mind. If she ever needed a person to debate a topic over, Jamie was her man. He was adventurous, and Annaca knew she could count on him to participate in new fantasies to play out if she was ever in a bind.

Since Annaca was on top, Jamie started to help her remove her clothing. He played with each part of her body that he exposed by kissing or licking it. While Jamie worked in one area, Tessa caressed Annaca from her hips to her supple breasts. Annaca had the attention of two partners, and it was a welcoming experience.

Tessa leaned up against the chaise lounge and began to lick and suck on Annaca's nipples; she slightly started to pinch them with her fingertips. Annaca moaned and started to grind into Tessa.

Annaca eased down to sit on Tessa's thighs as she used her fingers to massage Tessa inside and out. Tessa gripped Annaca's head every time she flicked her tongue. Annaca began to go faster. She wanted to hear Tessa climax. Annaca slid her fingers in and out of Tessa, hitting that g-spot. She pulled her fingers out of her occasionally to taste Tessa's sweetness.

Jamie was caressing Annaca, rubbing the inside of her thigh and moving his hands up to rub a circular pattern between her legs. He pulled his hand to his mouth and licked his first two fingers to wet them. Then he started stroking between her lips to get her juices flowing. Jamie continued to use fingers to stroke the inside of her while continuing to rub his thumb in a back-and-forth motion on her clit.

Annaca was pleasuring Tessa while being pleasured, and that was enthralling. Both girls were moaning and sighing with all the rubbing, and it was only a matter of seconds that they both came with loud groans.

Annaca and Tessa both reached out for Jamie to remove his blue jeans. Tessa got the button, and Annaca got the zipper. Jamie was ready and willing. His pants dropped to his ankles, and his boxers followed. He stood there with his pride and joy standing tall.

Both girls sat up on the lounge and pulled Jamie in front of them. Tessa reached out first. She looked him in the eyes as she began to run her fingertips up and down his shaft. She leaned forward and began to use her tongue to trace the head of his shaft, taking him into her heated mouth.

Annaca pulled Tessa's hair back as she played with her body, rubbing and massaging each part. Tessa increased her intensity with deep strokes. Jamie moaned with each mouthful.

Annaca tagged in and took her turn with Jamie. She grabbed his hips to position him, opened her velvety lips and began swirling her tongue around the head of his erect cock. She used her hand to stroke his throbbing tool with each pass of her tongue. Jamie pulled her long ebony hair back so he could watch her mouth tease him. Tessa encouraged Annaca to get up on her knees so that she was able to play with her. Tessa kissed her way down from Annaca's neck to her supple breasts.

They were so soft, and Tessa loved suckling her tight little rosy nipples. Tessa used her thumb to massage Annaca's button to get her wet as she slid her first two fingers into Annaca. Annaca paused for a moment during the first insertion. Her grip tightened slightly around Jamie's shaft as she felt a jolt of pleasure. Jamie was close to finishing early when Annaca stopped.

Tessa had Annaca melting in her hand. Annaca pushed Jamie back. She settled down on the chaise lounge with her legs spread, and Tessa was sandwiched between them. Tessa stood on her knees with her ass facing Jamie and her face in Annaca's crotch, licking, sucking, and fingering her. Jamie saw this as an opportunity to get behind Tessa. He licked his fingers to wet his target.

Tessa spread her legs apart slightly. She welcomed his gesture. Jamie gently inserted his throbbing cock, and she paused from Annaca to let out a high pitched moan. Annaca looked up and grinned as she watched him thrust into Tessa. Jamie's thrust made Tessa pause and clench down on Jamie. Annaca had a smirk as she felt Jamie's thrust through Tessa's fingers.

Tessa's moan vibrated through her tongue as it passed over Annaca's clit. Tessa wanted Annaca to shiver and shake beneath her, yet it was difficult as Jamie's hard cock continued to slam into her. Annaca was amused to watch the expressions wave across Tessa's face. She reached up and began to fondle Tessa's supple tits. Tessa's fingers quivered as they slowly massaged between Annaca's lips, sporadically rubbing her.

A few minutes passed by, and Annaca was eager to have Jamie's throbbing cock inside of her. Annaca wanted to bring Tessa to climax and yearned to be in the middle of the two. Tessa gingerly moved up so Annaca could switch places with her. Annaca turned around and put both hands down on the chaise lounge and bent over with her feet planted, flagging Jamie to enter her hot, tight wetness.

Tessa slid into the spot where Annaca was, eager to be finished by her sweet mouth. Annaca was dripping wet from Tessa's pleasuring. She was so ready to feel Jamie's throbbing tool glide inside of her. Jamie obliged by grabbing Annaca's hips and positioned her so he could plunge into her feverish wetness.

Moaning and gripping the lounge on either side of Tessa, Annaca let out a whisper, "Harder..."

With another thrust, Annaca raised her voice and demanded, "Give it to me harder! Pull my hair, smack my ass and give me all you got!"

Jamie, surprised by her demand, did as she wanted. He wrapped her hair around his left hand and pulled her hair toward him. Annaca's head whipped back as she moaned. Intrigued by her reaction, Jamie smacked her ass hard enough to leave a handprint. "Oooooh, Yes!" Annaca exclaimed. A tingling sensation went through Annaca with every thrust to her pelvic bone.

Annaca tried to concentrate as she sucked on Tessa's clit a bit faster. In between thrusts, she dipped her head to stick her tongue into Tessa. Her body tensed up as she was close to finishing. Jamie's thrusts were as hard as he could go, and the sound of his hips smacking Annaca's ass echoed across her flat. Tessa stretched to reach for Annaca's nipples. She pinched them a bit, and Annaca moaned.

She was so close to climax. Jamie's body began shaking with erratic thrusts, Annaca tightening her muscles around Jamie's rock hard cock, squeezing every last drop out of him as her climax hit. Tessa's muscles gripped Annaca's fingers and squeezed as she moaned in ecstasy. The three of them quivered and toppled onto the chaise lounge as they sighed deeply. Now exhausted yet still drunk, they all rolled onto the floor to feel the coolness of the wooden surface.

"Wow, I can't believe we just did that!" Annaca exhaled.

Tessa breathlessly sighed out, "That was amazing."

Jamie leaned back with a smile plastered on his face. He just got a fantasy he could check off his bucket list.

Chapter Six

Late Night Visitor

Warm autumn rain was falling gently all over the city. Most people avoided the rain, but Annaca loved the smell of it. Warm rain was a reminder of home comfort that she enjoyed. A breeze blew in through her open window as the three of them lay on the floor of Annaca's flat. That was an amazing encounter. A night she never thought was possible. It all started with a wink from a young red headed woman in her office and a little sex on the beach.

As they lay sprawled out and exhausted, another breeze through the window brought the fresh smell of the rain and drifting thoughts of Weston into Annaca's mind. It was only a moment, but she ached for his touch. Jamie was wonderful, but there was something about those firm hands stroking her body. His southern drawl and his gorgeous eyes flowed through her mind.

Annaca wondered if she would ever see him again. She closed her eyes as rain from the window gently fell on their bodies. She never imagined that her lustful thirst would take her to places like this. Just a taste of this pleasure and she needed more.

Later that morning, they woke up frantically from sleeping in. Panicked, they all scrambled to get dressed and head to their destinations of work. The storm had continued through the night and into the morning, soaking all who went outside. Annaca showed up at her office drenched to the skin and now freezing from the air conditioning in the office.

She shivered and went to her desk. Spending the day making phone calls to potential clients, her mind would drift in and out of flashes from the night before and then to images of Weston walking through her office door. She needed to see him again, craved for his body pressing up against hers. She could feel his hands caressing her body. His lips on her neck with his soft kisses.

Annaca was taking a slight break from her fantasies to concentrate on work. She was about to get behind, and that was not like her. With autumn upon the city, it was getting close to the holiday season. Business always got slow for the firm during the holiday season. Parties and gatherings will happen all over town for the next three months. Annaca was excited for the season, especially with the annual fall celebration.

Thousands of people came to the city to attend the festival. Several celebrations would take place throughout the entire city; music of all varieties, dancing in streets, the smell of freshly baked goods and best of all, the costumes. Each year, people would try to outdo their work from the year before. The creativity that people put into their costumes and decorations was legendary.

Annaca sat gazing out her office window, watching the rain fall and listening to the thunder crack and rumble. Occasionally, lightning would strike and scare the office people, but it was a normal autumn storm. It always rained at the beginning of fall. Storms terrorized the city as if they were cleansing the area before the upcoming holidays. It seemed never ending and would lighten up here and there, but the rain always came back.

Her office windows rattled as the thunder angrily grumbled through the sky. The sound could make a person nervous. The crack of the last thunder shook the building, and several people gasped. Annaca chuckled as the intrusive thought seeped into her mind of which roll of thunder and lightning would take down the building.

The last roll of angry sky vanished as the storm moved onto its next target. People started to relax now that the storm had moved on. Sighing with relief, Annaca started thinking about her costume for the celebration and wondering which one would be suitable for this year. Maybe she will go Victorian style with a gown that will turn heads. She wanted to grab attention as she walked by. Her mind started to wander into daydreaming about the festival and the touch from Tessa's tender fingers.

Annaca thought about finding another girl to take back to her flat, but only a girl. Any touch was desired, rather it be Tessa, Weston, Jamie... She imagined a woman's touch all over her body and leaned back in her chair. She wanted the smell and taste of an aroused woman as she felt her own body grow wet and excited.

Gently, she ran her hands down the sides of her thighs, imagining her hands were Tessa's. Tessa seemed to have a way with Annaca. The thought of Tessa had the ability to jumpstart Annaca's imagination. Shaking her head to snap back to reality, she sat up and started to gather her things to go home. She needed a hot bath and a strong drink.

It was the end of the day, and Annaca couldn't wait to get back to her flat. As she was leaving the firm, the rain started to pick back up again. The bus was pulling up to the stop outside of the firm. She scurried to the bus and hopped on. She watched the rain trickle down the windows as she leaned back in her seat. Her stop was ahead, and she wanted the warmth of a bath and a hot cappuccino to ease her mind.

The bus screeched to a stop, and the hydraulic sound of the doors made Annaca flinch. As she exited the bus, the thunder started to grumble. She shook her head and rushed to her flat. Skipping to the door of her home, she searched for her keys. Standing in front of her door, she turned the key to unlock it and open the bottom door. She climbed the stairs, and a wave of relief washed over her as her peace of mind stood in front of her.

As she walked into her flat, a strange idea changed her direction. She placed her stuff just inside the doorway and took her shoes off. Just like that, she turned around and went back down the steps. As she stepped back outside onto the sidewalk, she let the rain fall down on her. Instead of a bath, she chose a rain shower. Closing her eyes and tilting her face to the sky, she held up her arms and let the rain wash everything away.

The rain was cold yet refreshing. Memories of being in the country and standing in the rain flooded her mind. As a child, she could let it wash-away all of her cares. For a fleeting moment, she felt lighter and had no worries. Her body began to shiver; It was time to go back inside. She squeezed the rain from her long ebony hair, smiled and walked back inside. Ascending the stairs, she swore she could hear footsteps behind her.

Just as she turned around to close the door, Tessa was standing there. Annaca jumped at being startled. She wasn't expected company, but she welcomed the idea.

"I saw you as I was passing by and wondered if you would like some company?" Tessa asked.

Annaca smiled happily and replied, "Sure. I could use some company. Come on in."

As Tessa followed, she kept an eye on Annaca walking away. She remembered the night they had and got a tingle of excitement. The thought flooded her memory and was so close to being a repeated action. Just then, Annaca turned around and motioned for Tessa to walk past Annaca. Tessa ran her hand across Annaca's ass as she eased by.

She continued to draw a path around her hip, and down to Annaca's hidden jewel. Tessa wanted to taste her one more time. Annaca flinched with surprise but welcomed the touch. Tessa began swirling her fingers around Annaca's sweet spot, trying to entice her through her already soaked clothing.

Annaca grabbed Tessa's hand and looked her dead in the eyes as she pulled her into a kiss. Annaca finished the kiss with a nibble on Tessa's bottom lip. Tessa grinned because she knew she was going to get a moment with Annaca, alone. Taking Annaca by the hand, Tessa walked her backward to the chaise lounge. Tessa started stripping Annaca of her drenched clothing, which made them difficult to remove.

With a bit of help from Annaca, they were both bare, with goose bumps everywhere. Admiring Annaca's perky nipples, calling her mouth, Tessa leaned in and warmed one with her mouth. Annaca cradled her head and pulled her in tighter. A twinge of warmth jolted through Annaca's body as she pushed Tessa down onto the lounge. Tessa leaned back as Annaca mounted her.

She leaned down, crushing their lips together. Tessa held Annaca's hips as Annaca kissed her way down to the gem she wanted to suck on. Tessa shivered with each chilling kiss. Annaca's warm breath sent a twinge of excitement through her body. Annaca sucked in Tessa's clit into her mouth as she stoked her fingers in and out of Tessa. Everything began warm and tingle, Tessa was about to orgasm.

Annaca could feel her tighten on her fingers, so she drove her fingers in harder, making Tessa's body shutter. Annaca's hand warmed with Tessa's juices pouring out. She held the pressure to her g-spot, making sure Tessa finished. She pulled her hand out and used Tessa's wetness to lube herself up.

Tessa gingerly sat up to switch positions with Annaca. She wanted to return the pleasurable treat. Tessa straddled Annaca.

She pulled Annaca's hands up over her head and said, "Keep your grip on the edge of the lounge. It's my turn to have my way with you."

Annaca did as she was told; she found the instruction to be arousing. Tessa kissed her way down Annaca's body with an occasional flick of her tongue. Annaca quivered under Tessa with eagerness. Tessa reached Annaca's already engorged clit and gave it a quick flick with her tongue. Annaca trembled. She began slowly rocking back and forth with every stroke of Tessa's tongue.

Tessa slipped two fingers inside of Annaca to hit that pleasure button. The sensation made her let out a gasp of ecstasy. Tessa moved her other hand up Annaca's side so she could caress her breast, slightly pinching her nipple. Annaca's nails gripped into the lounge on the brink of explosion.

Annaca was moaning, "Oh god; yes! Right there, faster!"

Within seconds of hitting that sweet spot, Annaca's creamy juices trickled down Tessa's face and hand. Annaca was quivering and trying to push back. It felt so good, and she didn't want Tessa to stop.

Annaca fell backward onto the lounge, and Tessa sat up, leaned over and started kissing her way up to Annaca's neck, occasionally rubbing her clit to watch Annaca twitch and jump from sensitivity. Tessa looked into Annaca's eyes and smiled as if saying, *You're welcome.* Annaca grinned and pulled Tessa up into a long, deep kiss. That was exactly what she needed to relax and get her mind off of the man plaguing her mind.

Tessa, pleased with her work, laid beside her on the chaise lounge and curled up with Annaca. Annaca was freezing, so she sat up quickly to yank the knitted blanket that rested on the edge of the lounge, over her and Tessa. Annaca slowly started to drift off to sleep. She was satisfied for the moment.

Tessa wrapped her arms around Annaca's naked body and hugged her tight. She kissed her forehead and hoped for more nights like this. Annaca was a wild child, though. It wasn't easy to keep her pleased. As fantasies drifted through Tessa's mind, she fell asleep holding a beautiful woman for the night.

Chapter Seven

Fall Festivities

The sun shone through the window and woke the girls up. It was a wonderful night together, and they discussed the repeat of it over coffee. It was nice to wake up with someone for once. Tessa knew that Annaca liked her space, but an occasional visit would be welcomed. She wouldn't mind dating Annaca, but she had a feeling that Annaca was a free spirit and was far from settling down.

Knowing this, Tessa inquired about the occasional visits. Annaca grinned and was happy to hear it and agreed wholeheartedly. Annaca did want to see Tessa a bit, but nothing serious would come from the liaison. Annaca knew there was more to learn about her newfound obsession. She couldn't make up her mind. Did she want a girl or a guy or both to play the part in her fantasies? Annaca was excited to see where her adventures would take her.

The annual fall costume celebration was going on downtown. Annaca couldn't wait to see what the city had come up with this year. She loved to wander and watch the people. It was one of her favorite times of the year. There were so many young, alluring women and men all around the festival. Some were dressed up in their finest and elegant costumes. Others were more traditional. A few steampunk costumes meandered through the crowd.

Annaca admired the couples that waltzed around. There was one woman who looked regal in her costume. Annaca could not take her eyes off of her. A shimmering, iridescent floor-length gown with black lace trim swayed as she walked. A delicate black swirled mask covered her face but not her eyes. Her eyes sparkled in the glow of the flame-lit streetlights. The young woman was wearing a corset that gave her an hourglass figure. She mesmerized Annaca.

She was so fixated on her that Annaca didn't notice the gentleman who had walked up behind her. The gentleman's hands were strong and rather large. He had placed them over Annaca's eyes trying to get her to guess who he was. His essence was familiar and intriguing. He smelled of fresh rain and rugged cologne that sparked a deep sensual memory.

All of a sudden, she could feel the imaginary warmth of a brick wall behind her. It was Weston. He had made it back to town for the festival. She shivered with excitement and nervousness. Although she was a bit annoyed with him as well. No contact for all of this time.

"Surprise, I'm so sorry I didn't call. I have been held up with so much work at my parent's farm. Do you forgive me?" Weston asked sheepishly.

"Well, I should be quite angry with you. You left me at a rather delicate moment, and I felt it was my fault. You didn't even return my call or text message." Annaca stressed.

Bowing gracefully, Weston asked, "With my most sincere apologies, Ms. Annaca, will you please accompany me as my date for the festival?"

Annaca tried to look irritated as she smacked him on his shoulder. She couldn't stay mad at him, though. Grinning, Annaca accepted and took his arm with her lace gloved hand. The costume she wore was a dated Victorian-style dress of red crushed velvet and trimmed with black lace. Her ebony hair was styled with a carelessly messy bun and a small red velvet hat pinned to the bun to match her dress. Her royal blue eyes could pierce through the heart of anyone who looked into them. Weston occasionally glanced in her direction to admire her. She was gorgeous, and he just couldn't look away from her.

Weston's costume was a full tuxedo with a top hat made of black satin. He was gorgeous and looked like he just stepped off the red carpet. He had a long black cane with a silver knob at the top. Those devilish green eyes had Annaca swooning for another night with him. What's not to love about a man in a full tuxedo?

Weston knew he was astonishing to look at, as all attractive guys know. He was eye candy of the rarest form. How could she say no to the man who started all her desires of passionate lust? Even if it would be a short visit with him, she wanted to have him. Annaca wanted to finish what they started, and she wasn't taking no for an answer.

The two of them were admired by many as they walked through the city, receiving many compliments as they passed other couples. Annaca got her wish. People were watching her with Weston as if they were on parade. No one knew who the actual arm candy was. They were a gorgeous couple, but Annaca wanted him for his body, not his looks.

The other woman in the gothic gown had been completely forgotten the moment Weston appeared. Smiling occasionally up at him, she wanted to feel the touch of his hands. He was jaw dropping gorgeous. She had all of his attention and hoped he had the same craving for her. She had formed a plan to take advantage of her time with him if he didn't cut out on her again.

Across the way, a small six piece band was playing tango and waltz music. As they got closer, the sounds of a violin, trumpet, cello, clarinet, trombone and flute harmoniously played a waltz. Weston gestured toward the music, "Shall we?" Annaca blushed and let him lead her closer. Taking her hands, he bowed to her, and she accepted with a curtsy.

Weston slowly spun her around and brought her in to begin a two step. He didn't waltz, but he didn't need to. He charmed her with every step, occasionally twirling her around. The night was magical and felt like a dream. Most women would kill for a night like this.

"So, why did it take you so long to come back to town?" Annaca asked.

Weston sighed and replied, "I had to help my parents on the farm. We raise livestock, and my parents aren't as young as they used to be. That's where I got the idea for the ropes. Wrangling cattle isn't easy. I have found that nylon ropes seem to work a great deal better."

"That's office talk, I thought you said no office talk," grinned Annaca.

Weston shook his head and snickered, "True, I did say that. But, you did also ask where I had been."

"Fair enough, so how long are you staying this time?" Annaca inquired.

"Ouch, that was a jab," laughed Weston.

"I'm not sure. I won't be needed in the country for a little while. So, I guess a couple of weeks, unless I get an emergency call such as, fence broken, livestock out, you know, that sort of thing." Weston answered.

Thinking carefully, Annaca didn't want to run him off, but she had to ask. "What would you say about going back to my place?"

"I would like that very much, ma'am." Weston replied.

"I have something I would like to try with you, but it's a surprise." Annaca grinned.

"A surprise, huh? Well, darlin', lead the way. I'm up for a surprise." Weston replied.

He spun her around one last time. Dipped her down and kissed her, that long kiss she had ached for. Her lacy-gloved hand grazed his chin and caressed his face as she pulled him closer. When the kiss broke, he stood her up. Then he bowed to her. Weston thanked her for the dance and offered his arm to escort her.

She grinned up at him and wrapped her arm around his. They left the festivities like two teenagers about to cause some trouble and headed to a more secluded location of her choice. She wanted to live out a fantasy right now, and what a perfect time with all the excitement. Fantasies don't always go as planned, but the spontaneous treat would be well worth the try.

Weston decided he was going to put a twist in her plan. He had a few ideas of his own. Annaca seemed willing to try new things, and Weston hoped she would be willing. Curiosity made him wonder if he could put a bit of kink into their escapades. With a new adventure on the rise, he had to be gentle.

Questioning his abilities, he wasn't sure if he would scare her with his ideas. He did like rough, but he was hesitant since he hadn't had many partners. With all the farm work, he didn't get out much. He wasn't looking for anyone when he ran into Annaca. Stress relief from life was what he was after, and what better way to relieve stress than to have sex with an adventurous woman?

Chapter Eight

Center Stage

Knowing the theater was closed for maintenance and cleaning, Annaca wanted to be center stage with her fantasy. She hoped Weston was up for it. She wanted to get caught in the act. Semi-public places were becoming a theme for her sexual habits.

They arrived in front of the theater after the walk from the festival. Weston assumed that they were going to her flat. He reached for the entrance of her flat, and Annaca shook her head and said, "Not that way silly."

She coaxed Weston to follow her through the back entrance that she had braced open earlier that day, hoping to find another partner at the festival. She never dreamed it would be Weston, but he was her perfect idea of a willing participant in her show. They slipped through the door and left the brace just in case they needed a quick escape.

Weston was anxious about the theater stage, but Annaca was difficult to resist in that gown. He wanted to pick up where they had left off. He wanted to rip the dress down the center and spread it out, creating a blanket to lay her down on.

"M'lady, may I ask why we are here?" Weston inquired.

Annaca grinned and replied, "Well, you did promise to watch a movie with me, and I thought since you are here, why not put on our own production?"

Weston shook his head, realizing what she was asking for, and then a smile spread across his face. *Maybe this girl was going to be kinky after all*, he thought.

"Well, Ma'am, if that is what you desire, I mustn't keep a lady waiting." Weston replied.

He offered his hand to Annaca. As she accepted it, he pulled her in and spun her around and dipped her. As she was bent back, he kissed her gently. His lips were so soft, and his kiss was intoxicating. Gradually, Weston brought her back into a standing position. He entranced Annaca. She reached for his face as she pulled him in tighter.

His intoxicating scent drove her wild. Breathing him in as they kissed, she put her hands around his waist, plunging his hips into hers. She could feel a throbbing poke from below that told her he was ready to take her right there on the stage. They staggered up onto the stage as they continued to make out. Their hormones were high, and they wanted each other with a deep, aching hunger.

Weston paused their kissing to hunt for a cloth, sheet, or a curtain, anything to lay her down on. He didn't want to get her dress dirty. Just behind the main curtains of the stage, was a slightly torn heavy velvet burgundy curtain. Weston walked over and straightened it out so that he could lay it down so it wasn't just a hardwood floor beneath them.

But first, something caught his eye, a set of old golden yellow satin tiebacks that were next to the curtain. An idea popped into his mind, and he now had a surprise fantasy of his own. The thought was already there, but the opportunity hadn't presented itself until now. He couldn't waste his chance for this.

Weston pulled a blue and white handkerchief out of his pocket and smiled at Annaca and asked jokingly, "How would you like to be tied up? Would you consider some minor bondage?"

Annaca thought about it for a few seconds.

"Actually, I have never tried that before, can we? Do I need to give you a safe word?" She laughed jokingly.

Weston, amused by the idea, got up from the hardwood floor, walked over to her and led her back to the curtain he had laid out. Kissing her, he flicked the bandanna out, and gently tied it around her eyes.

"Is that too tight?" He whispered in her ear.

He helped her to sit down on the curtain, careful not to kneel on her gown.

Annaca took her gloves off and laid them there on the floor. She ran her hands over her eyes, feeling the fabric.

"No, it's just fine." She replied.

Weston reached for the tiebacks and set them next to him. He gently laid Annaca down on her back while raising her arms above her head. He straightened out the tiebacks and tied the satin around her wrists. The tiebacks restrained Annaca, so she had no major movement of her hands, only her fingers.

Her senses took over, and she could feel every touch and kiss that grazed her body. Weston scooted down and started at her ankles, inching the gown up as he kissed his way up to her thigh. Annaca shivered with each brush of his lips across her skin. Licking her lips and moaning slightly, she just had to lay back and take it. This was a new sensation for her. She was used to controlling the narrative.

Weston grinned with each excited noise she made. He enjoyed teasing her with each touch of his lips. His warm breath reached her thigh, and she felt a grating ache go through her whole body. Weston pulled her black lacy panties completely off and tossed them to the side. Her body told him she hungered for this.

He spread her legs further apart, enough to where he could get in between them. He licked his two fingers, inserted them. Gradually, he pulled back to rub her clit up and down, back and forth. With each tremble of her body, Weston would grin. As he was bent over, it was getting difficult to get to her, so he spread her legs further apart so he could lie down.

As he was about to lick her, he stopped and just let her feel his breath. Anticipation of his next move had her panting. His breath was warm but cool when he stopped. Gently blowing on her clit was revving her up even more. She wanted to feel his tongue. Or better yet, that rock-hard cock slamming into her.

Annaca giggled, "Wow, such a tease! How about we turn this around and I tie you up?"

Weston laughed and said, "We can try that later."

Annaca huffed, "Well then, I need something a little harder, maybe you could help me with that?"

Weston, amused by her comment, asked, "You really want it? Are you sure you want me inside of you, or would you like me to continue?"

He licked her once, and she squealed, "Okay, I really want that right now."

Weston snickered and continued to maneuver his tongue as if he were writing out his alphabet with his tongue. It was around the letter W that she pleaded with him for more.

Annaca begged again as he finished with Z, "Yes sir, I really need you inside of me now. I want to feel your throbbing cock thrusting into me. I know you are hiding it there in those suit pants."

Weston smirked and was more than happy to oblige. He took off his jacket and laid it next to her. Then he pulled his shirt from his pants, unbuckled his belt, unbuttoned his pants and slid the zipper down. He pulled his pants and boxers down to his knees, exposing his pulsing tool of pleasure. He stuck a finger into Annaca, swirled it around and pulled it out to use her juices to moisten his shaft.

He grabbed hold of her hips and hoisted her up into position. Massaging his member and aiming for her, he slowly slid in, and Annaca let out a loud passionate moan, "Oh gods, yes!"

She pulled her tied wrists to prop her head up, wanting to grab him and pull him in deeper. His shirt was damp with sweat, so he paused to remove it. His body glistened under the lights of the stage. The mixture of cologne and sweat filled the air. Annaca tried to reach for him, but he slipped through her fingers. Wanting more, she tried to grip his hips with her thighs. She despised the binds that kept her from digging into him.

With every thrust, Weston seemed to swell inside of her. She felt hot with fever. The more her juices flowed, the harder he would plunge into her. Gripping her hips, he leaned up, and stood on his knees to get a better angle. Her muscles squeezed so tight he couldn't hold out anymore. He exploded inside her, and she loved it.

He had hit the spot with every pump. Just one last squeeze and she was in pleasure heaven. Her muscles tightened around his shaft as he gave one last thrust. He quivered from head to toe. He slammed a hand against the stage to avoid collapsing on top of her.

Taking a few deep breaths, he leaned in and kissed her forehead. Droplets of sweat fell from his brow and landed around her. Gently, he licked the tip of her nose and then moved in for a deep, sensual kiss.

A few moments into the kiss and one of the maintenance guys walked through the side door. Startled and unsure of what he was seeing, he spoke up, "Not to interrupt, but ya'll can't be in here."

"If you would be so kind and clean up your, uh, mess when you are done... That'd be great, thanks!" He suggested.

Shaking his head as he walked back out of the side door, thinking, *I wish I had thought of that, wonder what the wife would say...*

Annaca was thrilled at being *caught* in the act. Bringing her hands to her face, she pulled up the bandanna with her thumbs to see a guilty look on Weston's face. She smiled sweetly at him and said, "Don't worry, we're not in trouble, but we probably should get out of here."

Weston nodded and sat up so he could remove her wrist binding. He pressed against the wooden theater floor to raise himself to a kneeling position. He reached for his shirt with one hand and pulled down her gown with the other. Annaca scooted back a bit to give him room to move around. Weston stood up and then ducked back down to grab his boxers and pants.

Annaca grinned and said, "We could always take the second act upstairs."

Weston smirked and said, "If that is what you desire, your wish is my command."

Annaca's eyes sparkled with another idea she had wanted to try.

They gathered their clothing and pulled themselves together enough to retreat to her flat. As they exited the theater, the maintenance guy caught their attention with a wave. They sheepishly waved back and headed to the entrance door of her flat.

Chapter Nine

Sweet Dessert

They ascended the creaky old steps that led to her flat. A solid oak door with a black skeleton key handle stood in front of them. It appeared mysterious to the basic eye. Annaca called it her escape from the rest of the world. The unique flat above the old theater gave her peace of mind from the noise of town. She could do whatever she wanted in her little piece of heaven.

Just above the door was a handcrafted sign that read, "Flat Heaven." Weston glanced up, reading the sign and asked, "Heaven, huh?"

Annaca smiled and replied, "Yes, it's my very own quaint escape, and I can show you heaven, right through that door."

With an exchange of grins and eye rolls, she unlocked the door and displayed the entrance to her flat. It was quiet and smelled of cinnamon twisted with sage. Each area of her flat had a unique fragrance. Between candles, decorative pieces, bookshelves, incense and air fresheners, her flat teased the senses.

A normal interior decorator would have a fit about how she designed her heaven, but it was a twist of country and Halloween all year long. Although Annaca appreciated city life, she was at home in her country decor. The only thing she was missing was a rain shower in the bathroom.

Weston was amused by her collection of books and dust collectors. He couldn't get a full picture of this young woman because she was all over the map. She seemed to have a little of everything. In his eyes, she was adorable with a kinky side. This wildcard of a woman was going to keep him busy. Secretly, he needed to know her completely.

Though unsure of his ability to keep the interest of said wildcard, he was eager to try with his southern country boy charm. He didn't really know what he could offer her except pleasure and decent company. Laying his jacket across her chaise lounge, he reflected on being downstairs on the stage.

Her body held his mind hostage. It would be difficult to escape her temptress ways. She was still in her gown, and it was complimenting to her lissome form. Walking gracefully around the flat, she picked up a few things here and there to return them to their rightful place. A seductive smile tugged at the corner of her mouth as a provocative idea formed.

A new kink was developing in her mind. The desire to create the scene of another fantasy was spinning in her thoughts. She had everything she would need to challenge his body to a new level of ecstasy. It was simple, but she had to strike now before he vanished again.

The mess was going to be worth the effort. Whipped cream, chocolate syrup, strawberries, handcuffs, a blindfold and a gorgeous man to lick clean. *What could go wrong there*? She wanted to test his senses this time, and she wasn't taking no for an answer. Annaca wanted to enjoy her dessert.

Grinning, Annaca placed her shoes by the door and asked, "Since we had dinner the last time we were together, how about dessert?"

Weston gave her a perplexed look. Annaca walked over to her refrigerator and pulled out the whipped cream, strawberries and the chocolate syrup.

Weston raised his eyebrow with intriguing thoughts of where this might go.

A twinge of excitement surged through his body, and everything about his muscular structure tensed up. This girl had his attention. She pushed to the next level through her fantasies, and he was happy to be her test subject.

Annaca placed her items next to the bed and then went into her jewelry box. Opening up a secret compartment, she pulled out a blindfold, a feather whip and a pair of shiny handcuffs.

"So, what do you think about it?" Annaca inquired as the cuffs swung around her finger.

Weston grinned and replied, "As long as I can hold the key, I'm up for almost anything."

"Shall we then?" Annaca asked.

Annaca sauntered over to the bed to remove her gown and reveal her matching set of undergarments. She pushed the gown onto the floor, sat down and patted the satin cover next to her while swinging the cuffs on her delicate fingers. Eyebrow raised, Weston felt compelled to remove every article of clothing. Annaca watched his uncanny striptease as she waited patiently for him to come to her. Weston was about to walk to her, only in his boxers until Annaca shook her head and said, "Um, no, those too,"

Grinning like a fool and shaking his head, Weston again did as she asked. He pulled them down to show every inch of his body. Gorgeous, rippling muscles with a Cheshire cat grin stood in front of her.

"That's better. Come on over and lie down for me, please. I promise I won't be too rough." Annaca smirked.

Weston returned the smile with a wink. "Promise? My safe word phrase is, please, don't stop." He joked.

He waltzed over to her bed, crawled around her and flopped down behind her with his hands propping his head up. She turned around and mounted him. She pulled his hands from behind his head and opened the cuffs. He gave her a goofy grin and asked about the key for safekeeping. She paused for a second, pulled her hair back and revealed the key's hidden location.

She had it on a simple chain that hung around her neck, with the key resting in her cleavage. Since the key was so close, he didn't panic. Annaca proceeded to guide his hands to the post she intended on cuffing him to. He didn't resist her. He wanted this eagerly.

His hands were cuffed, and a black satin blindfold covered his emerald eyes. Each time he moved his muscles bulged and flexed. His bronze body lay across her crimson satin bedcover. She admired all of his features. Thinking she had just plucked him out of a magazine and placed him on her bed.

She took the whip that had ruby red feathers on one end and leather strings flowing from the other. She wanted to watch him squirm and wriggle. With the feathers, she traced each muscle from his chest down to the perfectly formed V cut. Watching each muscle tense with the grazing of the feathers.

His pulsating cock twitched as she guided the feathers across the tip and down the shaft. Returning the favor from the stage, she leaned down and gently blew on the head. It stood at attention from the touch of her lips. She swirled her tongue up and down his shaft and around the head. Weston groaned with unbridled passion. He had been waiting for his turn on the pleasure tour.

Annaca wanted to sweeten the taste, so she sprayed whipped cream on the tip. She poured a bit of chocolate syrup onto her fingertips and massaged his shaft. Ready for her dessert, she started at the top, opening her mouth to take it all in. The warmth of her mouth was exhilarating. Using her tongue to massage his shaft, she had his whole body quaking. The sweet taste in her mouth was creamy with a chocolate chaser. Pulling back, she licked her lips and sucked her fingers clean.

She had his undivided attention and wanted to test out a new trick she had learned from a tantric sex video. She was unsure how he would respond, but they were trying a few different tactics tonight. While she kept his attention with her mesmerizing mouth, she placed her thumb at the base of his member and wrapped her first two fingers around the bottom of his shaft. The pressure from her thumb increased his moans. Slowly, she moved her fingers to wrap around his balls, and she applied a bit of pressure just under his sac.

The sensation sent Weston's whole body into erratic trembles. He was trying so hard not to thrust. "Oh, fuck," he whimpered out.

Annaca continued to intensify the one sensation and applied a little more pressure to the other two pressure points. Weston's body shuddered with every downward stroke of her mouth. She could feel the blood coursing through his cock. It was only a matter of seconds. Exploding in her mouth, she continued to take him all in. It was a bitter-sweet taste added to the chocolate and cream.

She sat up, grinned at him and reached for her nightstand bottle of water, washing everything down. Weston drew in deep sighs of relief while quivering with ecstasy. He had never experienced a sexual act so intense.

"How did you... Where did you..., nevermind, don't tell me." He stammered out.

Annaca continued to drink her water, pleased with her work.

"I know I just had dessert, but I'm starving. How about you?" She asked.

Weston, amused by her question, replied, "I have worked up an appetite. What's open this late around here? And before you even think about it, I'm paying. It's the least that I can do."

"Well, there is Chinese down the block or pizza," Annaca replied.

"Dealer's choice," Weston said.

Annaca had thought about it for a few seconds. "Chinese?" She asked.

Weston shrugged and said, "Sure."

Annaca grabbed her cell phone and ordered a box of shrimp fried rice and beef lo mein.

Weston was still sprawled out on the bed, hands still cuffed.

"In order to actually eat, you might have to release your prisoner. Unless you plan on feeding me." He hinted.

Annaca giggled, "Well, at least I would know where you are."

"True, but then I wouldn't be able to please you after dinner with a second round," replied Weston.

Their playful banter went on for a few minutes until there was a knock at the door. A voice outside the door hollered, "Food delivery."

They both looked at each other, and Weston, who looked worried about being seen in his current state, asked for the keys.

"Please hurry, I don't want to be seen like this by the delivery person," Weston pleaded.

Annaca laughed, grabbed her robe off the chair next to her dresser and threw it over him while tossing the keys just out of reach. She grabbed a baggy t-shirt from her dresser and put it on as she ran to the door to receive their food and had a huge smile on her face the whole time.

The delivery guy was maybe five foot six inches tall, tan, with dark brown hair and light brown eyes. He had a big cheesy grin on his face when Annaca opened the door with only her shirt on. He handed over the order and asked, "Another long night of work, Ms. Annaca?"

Annaca looked over her shoulder for a moment. Then she turned back, grinned and replied, "Something like that. Thank you. You keep the change."

Annaca placed all the food onto her small round table in her version of a dining room and walked back over to the bed. Weston was still handcuffed to the bed, looking awkward.

Annaca giggled and apologized for leaving him like that.

He seemed a little upset but thankful once she released him. He got up and grabbed his boxers and asked for a wet cloth to remove the residue of chocolate syrup and whipped cream. Annaca went into her bathroom and shortly came back with a damp dark blue washcloth. She handed it to him with a smirk and watched him struggle to clean up and put his boxers on.

He didn't want to be naked on her cold dining chair. They both took a seat at the table and started eating and joking around.

"So, since you have practically stayed the night, are you crashing with me tonight at least?" Annaca asked.

Weston stopped mid-bite and looked up. "I will have to get going in the morning. I got word that they need me back at the farm."

Annaca smiled, but quickly turned to a frown. "I thought you were in town for a couple of weeks?"

"I was, but I have some errands to run in town in the morning and then I have to head back." Weston replied.

They finished eating, and Annaca cleaned up the table and put the leftovers in the fridge. She walked over to her linen chest and pulled out a new comforter along with a clean set of sheets and set them on her chaise lounge. She pulled her dirty bedding off and tossed it on the floor, to be dealt with in the morning.

Shaking out her fitted sheet, Weston tried to help her get the bed set up for actual sleep. They laughed about the struggle they were having with the fitted sheet. Annaca pulled the last corner down and grabbed her top sheet and comforter off the chaise lounge. She shook them out together and laid them across the bed.

Annaca looked at Weston and asked, "Would you like to accompany me in the shower?"

Weston looked up at Annaca and walked right over to her. "Do you think I am dressed for such an occasion?"

Annaca smiled and removed the blindfold from around his neck and dropped his boxers with her fingers, "Now, I believe that you are indeed ready."

Weston smirked and hoisted her up. Annaca wrapped her legs around his waist and kissed him while holding onto his strong shoulders. She pointed to the bathroom, and he carried her while gently kissing her neck.

Entering the bathroom, he gradually let her down. Placing her feet first on the tile floor. His hands guided her t-shirt above her head, and then he slung it into her laundry basket in the corner.

"Two points to the shooter," Annaca cheered.

Annaca gasped. "I completely forgot about the strawberries!"

Weston shook his head at the realization she had.

"I think we can worry about the strawberries later. I have something else in mine." He replied.

Annaca quickly turned around and started the shower water, internally thinking she was a space cadet for the random outburst. They climbed into the shower, letting the water rain down on them. She reached for a washcloth and then held it under the water.

Weston pulled the washcloth from her fingers. He lathered it up with soap as he washed her back, slipping down her ass cheeks and around her hips. Slowly, he ran his hands down the outside of her thighs and then up. Feeling his way to Annaca's core.

Weston casually massaged up and down between her lips. He could feel her arousal. Inserting one finger in to use juices to lubricate the rest of her. He began rubbing in a circular motion and then up and down, trying to coax her to whimper at his touch.

Annaca placed her hands on the shower wall to brace herself. He knew what buttons to push to get her in the mood. He wanted to give her a quick orgasm. She was so much tighter when she got off first. Weston continued to rub and massage her until she climaxed with a shuttering moan.

He quirked a smile as he stroked his cock to full potential. Annaca was still against the wall, squeezing her muscles to hold on to that fleeting orgasm. She spread her feet apart a bit and waited for him. Weston was throbbing with anticipation to enter her. Guiding his rock-hard cock with his fingers, he found her sweet spot and gently slid in.

She was so hot and wet. Gripping her hips, he glided in and out of her with increased speed. Annaca let out a load moan, and Weston couldn't hold out anymore. He came with a violent shudder that shook him, as his gripping hands shook her hips, making her butt jiggle.

This had been such a long and pleasurable day for both of them. They let the water wash all the sweat and other sticky substances away from their bodies. Annaca took the washcloth and proceeded to gently caress his body while covering him in suds. He occasionally kissed her tenderly. There was still a twinkle of lust in his green eyes. He wanted so much more of her yet again; he would have to leave for a while.

They finished their shower and walked out of her tiny bathroom, in towels. Annaca flopped down on the bed, hoping for some warm cuddling time. Weston grinned and shook his head. He gathered up his clothes and slowly put them on.

Annaca perked up and asked, "What's up? I thought you were going to stay the rest of the night with me?"

Weston pouted a bit and replied, "Well, I have basically done that. The sun is rising, and I have to get back. I'm truly sorry, but I can't stay any longer."

Annaca's smile faded. She got up from the bed and walked over to him, putting her hands around his waist. She smiled up at him, hoping for a kiss goodbye at least. He looked down at her and kissed her forehead.

Annaca grimaced as she said, "How about a proper kiss since I have no clue when I will see you again."

Weston shook his head and said, "Of course. I wouldn't leave without a taste of those sweet lips one more time."

He placed a hand on each side of her face as he leaned down to kiss her one last time. This kiss made Annaca rise up on her tiptoes to get closer to him. His lips were tender and warm. She didn't want to see him go. She wouldn't admit how much she liked him, though. It was too soon for something like that. She still had time to play, and she had a feeling he wasn't going to be back anytime soon.

The kiss ended with Weston pulling away first. Annaca frowned, yet she understood.

He smiled at her and said, "Don't worry, I'll be back soon."

Leaning in, he kissed her lips gently and then her forehead. He pulled away from her grasp and headed for the door. Annaca stood there for a moment before she rushed him and pinned him to the door.

"I'm not ready for you to go. One more genuine kiss and I promise to let you leave." She said.

He smirked. "Okay, but I really do, have to go. I have got to run my errands, and I will see you soon."

He grabbed hold of her, spun her around and dipped her over. With one hand behind her head, he pulled her into a kiss that would be on her mind for a long time. He stood her back up while still passionately kissing her.

When he pulled out of the kiss, Annaca did as she promised. She let him walk out of her door. Just before he closed the door, he gave a little wave of goodbye, and just like that he was gone again.

Chapter Ten

Fountain Play

It had been some time since Annaca had last seen Weston. He had a nasty habit of keeping her waiting. She knew it was for a good reason, but she wanted to see him. His family needed his help, and she still had no clue where they were located. All she could think about were his emerald green eyes staring into hers and that last kiss she could still feel on her lips.

He was able to take her to a whole new level of pleasure and quench her sexual thirst. He had what she wanted, and she needed more of his body, his touch and, most of all, she missed his kiss.

Trying not to be crazy or obsessed with Weston, she kept herself busy with work, friends and other escapades. Occasionally she found someone or something to occupy her time, but she often daydreamed of her time with Weston.

Carlene, her best friend, had invited her out for drinks and was excited to hear about her adventures. Carlene was a hairstylist and always loved a good story. She usually heard everyone's drama while they sat in her chair. Hair stylists are therapists of a special breed. Strangers would spill their life stories in her chair and then say, "I don't know why I told you all of that."

Most folks don't mind, plus it's a good way to keep up on the gossip of the town. Carlene enjoyed a good story from a client. She preferred the simple life of work, errands and then home. Carlene was a bookworm, like Annaca, with a love for romance novels. She had a few good friends, but Annaca always had the juicy sex stories to share. Carlene could live vicariously through Annaca without the stress of actually dating anyone.

Annaca and Carlene met up at Makko's. The restaurant was full, so they settled for a seat at the bar. Of course, Jamie was working there, and he kept smiling and winking at Annaca.

Carlene picked up on it and asked, "What that was all about."

Annaca blushed as she replied, "Well, you remember me telling you about the night I met Tessa? Well, our bartender joined in and we ended up having a threesome. I had a blast with them, and I look forward to trying that again."

She continued, "Jamie is absolutely adorable. He has always had my attention when I come here, but I don't want to settle down or anything."

She paused for a moment. "I doubt that I will hear from Weston again... And, Jamie is always available..."

"Girl, when are you going to tell him the truth… that you are head over heels for him?" Carlene asked.

Annaca shrugged her shoulders and said. "I don't think I will ever be able to tell him. That is if I ever see him again. He's always disappearing. It's almost like he only shows up when he is in the mood for something kinky."

Carlene grinned at her and shook her head. "One of these days you are going to have to speak up. You can't be mad at the man if you don't tell him anything. He will come back around; maybe he will even stay for a while. What would you do then?"

Annaca thought for a moment and replied with a smirk, "I would cuff him to my bed and never let him up again."

They both laughed loudly enough to catch the attention of the bar. Carlene ordered another drink as she waited to hear more about Annaca's escapades. She knew how Annaca behaved, and she lived for her stories.

Annaca tossed around a few thoughts in her head as she thought about Weston and her night with Tessa. The sexual heat of those events flashed through her mind. Just as she thought about Tessa, the memory of their last encounter washed through her mind. It sent a tingle through Annaca's body and seemed to be fate.

Tessa walked up behind the girls and took a seat next to Annaca at the bar. Annaca turned to see who had sat next to her as shock flashed across her face. She couldn't believe that Tessa was here. With a deep breath and a toothy grin, Annaca began to say hello, but Tessa beat her to it.

"Hey there, long time no see," Tessa said with a wink.

Fantasizing about Tessa, Annaca replied, "I was just thinking, I mean, talking about you."

"Well, it's always nice to be thought of often," Tessa replied.

Blushing, Annaca stuttered out, "I'm being so rude, Tessa, this is Carlene. She's my best friend."

Carlene and Tessa smiled at each other and shook hands. Simultaneously, they said, "Nice to meet you."

The girls started talking among themselves about life and general topics. Occasionally they would look up and admire their view of the bartender. They enjoyed their drinks and kept a watchful eye on Jamie. He wore a pair of tight Wrangler blue jeans with a white button-down shirt.

Jamie would grin every time he would mix a drink for Tessa and Annaca. The girls found it funny because they could read it all over his face. He was hoping for another fantasy night with two or possibly three women. *What man could resist a night with alluring women and pleasure*? He tried to hint at the topic, but the girls kept turning him down.

The girls talked and drank the night away, closing down the bar. It had become an unintended girl's night out that ended with three drunken women laughing the entire way out the door. Jamie excelled at his job again. He may have even over-poured a few drinks in hopes of having another go around with Tessa and Annaca.

As the girls stood outside of Makko's talking and laughing, Tessa leaned over and whispered in Annaca's ear, "Would you be interested in some company tonight?"

Annaca smiled and nodded. Carlene already knew that the plan had been set and this was her exit. She hugged Annaca, kissed her cheek and said her good nights.

She then hugged Tessa and said, "Nice to meet you. Have a wonderful night."

Annaca blushed and waved as Carlene headed to her vehicle. Tessa put a hand around Annaca's waist, and they turned to wave to Jamie. Jamie smiled at the girls and then gave a fake pouty face because he knew he was going to be left out of this adventure.

Before they walked away to the flat, Tessa placed her hands around Annaca's face, pulling her in close for a deep kiss. Annaca hungrily returned the kiss and placed her hands around Tessa's hips, pulling her body into hers. She needed some physical attention, and Tessa was about to hit the spot.

Pulling out of the kiss for a moment, Annaca made eye contact and asked, "Where would you like to go? We can go to my flat, or we can go to a new location."

Tessa swayed her hips with Annaca's and thought for a moment. "Well, we could go back to your place, or we could go anywhere you would like."

Annaca smiled. "I may have an idea. It might be a little risky. We may get caught."

"What do you have in mind?" Tessa inquired.

Annaca grinned and started pulling Tessa toward town. She had a very high-risk place in mind, and she was just drunk enough to try it out.

They walked and staggered for three blocks until they came to an open plaza with a giant fountain in the center. The pool around the fountain was easily three feet deep with different colored lights changing through the water streams of the fountain. The gray stones had flecks of shells that glistened in the surrounding light.

Tessa pulled Annaca in close to her and asked, "Are we going for a cold swim to sober up?"

Annaca blushed as she answered, "I figured we could warm each other up before and after."

Annaca leaned in and kissed Tessa with desire. Gently, she ran her hand up Tessa's shirt, caressing her side. Tessa shivered from her icy touch and grabbed Annaca's ass, pulling her back into her eager body. Annaca grinned and slipped her fingers under Tessa's bra, caressing her breast and gently pinching her nipple to feel it perk up in her fingertips.

Annaca loved how Tessa's body felt. Her skin was smooth. She lifted her shirt up along with her lacy ivory bra to display her breasts. Leaning down, she caressed her nipple with her tongue, gently suckling to feel Tessa's body twitch from the warmth of Annaca's lips enveloping. Annaca moved her other hand from Tessa's back to the ridge of her waistline.

Grazing her hip to the button of Tessa's pants, Annaca slid her fingers into Tessa's pants, past her satin panties and gently separated her lips to massage her gem with her fingers. Tessa let out a deep sigh. Annaca was getting wetter with each sound Tessa made. Annaca pulled her hand back and sucked on her fingers to moisten them so she could entice Tessa further.

Tessa's body was shivering from the sensation. Since they were both quite drunk and unstable, Annaca walked Tessa backward to sit her down on the edge of the fountain. She wanted to taste Tessa and return the favor from the night in the rain.

Tessa removed her jacket and laid it down so she could sit down. Annaca unbuttoned Tessa's pants and tugged them down to her thighs. Annaca took off her jacket and laid it at the base of the fountain so she could kneel down facing Tessa. Once on her knees, she looked up at her, grinning. Tessa smiled, placed her fingers around the back of Annaca's neck to pull her in for a kiss.

Eagerly, Annaca pulled Tessa's panties down. Annaca pulled out of the kiss and grinned up at Tessa. "I want to hear you moan."

Tessa giggled, "If you do what I think you are about to do, I'm going to be screaming your name."

They both laughed as Annaca moved her hands across Tessa's supple skin to separate her lips and display her deep pink clit. Using her right thumb, Annaca massaged Tessa's gem. Tessa's body jolted with every touch of Annaca's fingers.

While massaging Tessa's clit with her thumb, Annaca inserted her index finger, feeling the warmth of Tessa's juices. Tessa let out an intense sigh of pleasure. She was eager to feel the heat of Annaca's tongue. Tessa laced her fingers through Annaca's hair, pulling it back out of her face. Annaca knew what she wanted and smiled to herself as she was eager to please.

Annaca leaned in and slowly lifted her thumb to suck in Tessa's clit. Tessa's grip tightened around Annaca's head. Annaca released her suction and take a breath. She placed her hand to her mouth and sucked on her two first fingers and then, gently inserted them into Tessa as far as she could. Tessa groaned loudly enough that it echoed through the plaza. Annaca leaned in, and Tessa could feel her warm breath against her.

Using her tongue, Annaca swirled and teased Tessa's clit. Annaca's fingers gently rubbed in and out, applying pressure in all the right spots. Annaca wanted to intensify the sensation with pressure to her g spot. Tessa's body was trembling beneath Annaca.

She was so close to climax. Tessa pulled Annaca's head in tighter. Annaca inserted her fingers until she felt a textured center and then sucked hard on Tessa's clit. Tessa's head flung back, and she whimpered out, "Oh god, right there! Don't stop!"

Tessa's voice echoed through the plaza with her resounding pleasure. Tessa's body shuddered with her orgasm, clenching her muscles. Annaca continued to hold in place as Tessa's juices covered Annaca's hand. With one final flick of her tongue, Annaca teased Tessa. Tessa jumped and sighed with pleasure. "That was exhilarating. I have never done this in full public before." Tessa whispered.

Annaca smiled up at her and then laid her head in Tessa's lap. Tessa stroked Annaca's hair as she tried to catch her breath.

While the girls were enjoying each other, an officer was making his nightly rounds and heard them. Curiosity caused him to investigate the sounds echoing through the plaza. As he rounded the corner to enter the center of the plaza, he saw the girls sitting at the fountain. Assuming they were drunk, he started to walk toward them to shoo them home. The closer he got, the more he saw. He cleared his throat to get their attention.

"Ladies, isn't it a bit cold to, uh, be out this late?"

The girls both jumped at being startled. Annaca stood straight up, and when she did, Tessa lost her balance and fell straight into the fountain pool! Tessa flailed and splashed around as Annaca tried to rescue her friend.

Now freezing from the icy water, Tessa shot up for a deep breath of air. With her pants still around her ankles, she wobbled as she attempted to exit the fountain. All three of them were quite embarrassed. At the sight of Tessa, the officer quickly turned around. Tessa scrambled to pull her wet pants back on and crawl out of the pool.

Shivering, she sat down on the edge of the pool. Annaca felt horrible and quickly grabbed both of their jackets to place around Tessa.

"We're so sorry sir, we were only having a bit of fun," Annaca explained.

The officer shook his head and held back a laugh as he said, "I'm sure that was punishment enough for your friend. Maybe you two should head home before she freezes to death."

The girls both nodded and scurried out of the plaza back to Annaca's flat. The officer shook his head and couldn't wait to tell the guys back at the station.

The girls rushed to the flat above the theater. Embarrassed and freezing, Tessa asked, "Can I crash with you tonight?"

Annaca nodded and replied, "of course. It's my fault this happened, I'm so sorry. Let's get you warmed up."

Annaca pushed for Tessa to strip out of her wet clothes and found a pair of fuzzy sleep pants, socks and a sweatshirt for Tessa to wear.

"Tessa, go ahead and get under the covers, I'll be right there," Annaca suggested.

Annaca quickly changed into a matching set of flannel pajamas. Tessa was still shivering as she changed out of her wet clothes. She pulled back the cover and snuggled into Annaca's bed.

Annaca turned on a movie for background noise and walked over to her bed. She felt horrible about Tessa falling into the pool. She climbed into her bed and snuggled up with Tessa, hugging her and rubbing her arms. Annaca squeezed her and kissed her cold forehead.

"I'll warm you up." Annaca said.

It didn't take long for both of them to fall asleep. Tessa fell asleep to the sound of Annaca's heartbeat. Annaca wrapped her arms around her and welcomed the comfort of Tessa asleep on her chest.

The next morning, Annaca opened her eyes and yawned. She smiled to herself as she held Tessa in her arms. She kissed her forehead gently and whispered, "Good morning, how do you feel?"

Tessa stretched and looked up at her. "I feel warmer, thank you."

Both girls rolled away to stretch out on their backs, staring at the ceiling of Annaca's flat. Annaca stretched her arms above her head and yawned, then clasped her hands behind her head. Tessa wanted to take advantage of Annaca being so close. She rolled onto her side and looked at Annaca with a grin.

"What?" Annaca giggled.

"Well, I don't want to waste this moment with you. I want to properly thank you for saving me and warming me up." Tessa replied.

Running her hand up Annaca's side, Tessa reached for her breast and caressed it through her flannel pajama top. Annaca sighed. With her hands behind her head, Annaca's skin shone through the gaps in her top. The triangle gap at the bottom framed her adorable belly button. Tessa couldn't help but stare at her body. She was gorgeous.

Tessa massaged Annaca's breast and then slipped her fingers into the top gap of Annaca's flannel. Rubbing Annaca's nipple between her two fingers, Tessa pulled the gap to expose her perky nipple. Leaning in, she caressed it with her warm tongue, gently sucking it into her mouth. Annaca felt a twinge between her legs that sent a shock down to her toes. Tessa ran her hand down Annaca's body and into her flannel bottoms.

Tessa slid her hand between Annaca's thighs to spread them. Annaca wrapped her foot around Tessa's leg and pulled her on top of her. Tessa straddled Annaca, but slid back enough to reveal her whole torso. Annaca smiled up at Tessa, pulling her hands from behind her head to run her hands up Tessa's thighs. Tessa grinned down at Annaca and said, "I'll take that as a yes."

Annaca blushed and nodded.

Tessa unbuttoned Annaca's top so she could see and taste her supple breasts. She leaned in, rubbing the left one while sucking on the right. Annaca tugged at Tessa's bottoms, pulling them down to expose her enough that Annaca could play while Tessa teased her nipples. Annaca was amused to see Tessa flinch each time she would hit the right spot. Men can do a wonderful job at getting a girl off, but a girl knows what a girl wants. Annaca knew how to please both.

Tessa started rocking back and forth with the motion of Annaca's fingers. *There's nothing like morning sex,* Annaca thought. Annaca reached for Tessa's right hand and guided it to her center. Tessa understood and reciprocated the attention. Tessa licked her fingers for lubrication and gently slid them into Annaca. Annaca moaned from the sensation and gripped Tessa's hips.

She wanted deeper penetration. Tessa leaned in for a deep kiss, massaging Annaca's tongue the way she would tease her clit. Annaca tightened her muscles and tilted her hips upward. Tessa pushed a bit harder to give Annaca that deep hit that she wanted. Tessa hit at just the right angle. Annaca was in ecstasy.

She came with a force that made her entire body shudder and almost fold in half, knocking Tessa backward. After a few moments that seemed to last an hour, Annaca flopped back and pulled Tessa down with her. She flipped her over to where Annaca was on top. Annaca sighed and leaned back down for a satisfying kiss.

"I do believe that you are on fire now. There is nothing cold about you anymore. I'm very sorry that you ended up in the pool, though." Annaca apologized.

Tessa laughed and replied, "It is okay. It will be a great story to laugh about later."

Both girls grinned at each other, kissed a deep, passionate kiss and got up to get their day started. Annaca sashayed into her kitchen to prep a pot of coffee. She pulled out two mugs as she smiled about the night before.

"Hey, Tessa, would you like a cup of coffee to warm up?" Annaca inquired.

Tessa shook her head and replied, "Sure, as long as it doesn't require me to be in the fountain again. Hey, can I hang on to these clothes for a day? I really need to keep a spare set of clothes in my bag when I hang out with you."

Annaca nodded as she tidied up around her flat. Annaca sipped her coffee as she picked up a book and placed it back on the shelf. Feeling completely satisfied for the moment. What an amazing memory to add to her sexual journey. Tessa seemed to be her favorite female to experiment with at new locations.

Tessa finished her cup of coffee. She rinsed out her mug and stuck it in the sink. She needed to get home and get her place in order. Tessa had to be at work soon, though she didn't want to leave.

Tessa hung her head and walked over to Annaca. "I have to go; I've got to get to work." She said.

She motioned with a come here finger for Annaca to come closer.

Annaca stepped closer as Tessa grabbed her waist and pulled her in tight. Tessa turned Annaca to the wall next to the door and pinned her so she could kiss her deeply, with a goodbye kiss. Pulling back, she could still taste her coffee kiss.

"Until next time?" Annaca asked.

Tessa nodded and grinned.

"Of course, but next time, I choose the location. I can only imagine what that officer thought." Tessa teased.

They both laughed and said their goodbyes. Annaca smacked Tessa on the ass as she walked out her door.

"Definitely! There will be a next time." Annaca said while biting her lip and watching Tessa leave.

Chapter Eleven

Fair Game

The traditional holidays like Thanksgiving and Christmas had passed, and everyone was prepping for the New Year's Eve festival in the center of town. Annaca still hadn't heard from Weston, and she was starting to worry. She was excited about the festival, though. New faces all around in the cold crisp air.

Another year had come to an end, and hope for many floated in the air, disguised as snow. Couples were all walking about the town all snuggled up and loving on each other. The cold air seemed to bring people together, and then cause them to be irritable when the snow lasted past March.

The city was buzzing with New Year's cheer. Annaca was missing her country visitor, who showed up when he wanted to. She understood the reason, but a night with him would definitely jump her New Year into a wonderful start.

Annaca walked around town to see the decorations. She stopped at her favorite coffee shop to say hello to the cashier, Trent. He was a cutie with a country-boy smile. But he was a bit too young for her.

"How are you, Trent?" Annaca asked.

"I'm alright. I can't complain, there's no one here to listen." Trent snickered.

"Well, I'll have my usual, a large Columbian coffee with sweet cream topped with whipped cream, please." Annaca smiled.

"You never change up your order. Well, I do have some good news to share. I finally got my dream truck. It's a black '78 Ford F150 with original black interior. It has the original V8 motor with a four-speed, manual transmission. I got some work to do on her, but she's in great shape. Maybe I can take you out for a spin sometime?" Trent blushed.

"I would love that. I haven't been dirt road riding in forever." Annaca admitted.

They continued to chit-chat for a few moments until Trent's manager walked over with a scowl on his face.

"Yes, she's cute. But you have a job to do." His manager stated.

Annaca blushed and said, "I'll catch you next time, Trent. Call me when you want to take that truck out for a spin."

Annaca smiled to herself as she walked out of the coffee shop. She continued down the street, where there were smells and sounds all around from the festival. She secretly hoped Weston would surprise her again, but she wasn't keeping her hopes up. Although, he did tend to show up when she least expected him to.

Annaca stopped to lean against an old antique shop wall to enjoy her coffee and people watch for a moment. Snow flurries breezed by, and she got a shiver. She was ready for spring and warmer weather.

As she glanced around, there was a man staring in her direction. At first she thought nothing of it, but his stare became more intense. She was uneasy yet intrigued by this man. He was attractive in a city sense with a country style. Shaggy, mousy, brown locks of hair swayed across his face in the crisp breeze.

His piercing blue eyes seem to see right through her. He stood about six foot, maybe an inch or two taller. What caught her attention was the athletic build he was sporting. A tight pair of blue jeans, a baby blue, long sleeve, button down shirt, an open camouflage heavy jacket, Cowboy work boots and a backward baseball cap that was failing to keep his locks under control.

Her wild imagination dove into a brief fantasy of him walking over to her. Flashing a grin at her, while pinning her to the brick wall and leaning in for a kiss. He placed his hand on her cheek to feel her delicate skin while his other hand propped him up on the wall. His lips were warm and wet, pressing against hers.

Annaca reached for his face and could feel his five o'clock shadow under her fingers. She advanced her hands to the inside of his jacket to feel the heat of his body. His chest was muscular with a natural feel. He didn't have the chiseled abs, but he was real. He had actual meat on his bones, and his ass looked damn good in a pair of tight jeans.

Now she couldn't help but return the gazing stare. It seemed like he read her thoughts because he did in fact walk over and flash a big smile.

"I couldn't help but notice, that someone was stupid enough to leave you out here by yourself for the festival. Are you waiting for someone?"

Annaca blushed, "I was hoping to run into a friend or someone I knew, but it would seem I'm out of luck on that."

"Well, let me be your friend for the evening. My name is Austin, and I couldn't help myself. I had to meet you." He said.

Annaca grinned and replied, "Well, it is nice to meet you, Austin. My name is Annaca. Are you from the city or just visiting for the festival?"

Grinning, Austin replied, "I was hoping that my date was going to show, but I think I got stood up. Would you like to be my date for this evening's festivities?"

Annaca blushed. "Well, sure, why not. We both have been *stood up.*"

Austin offered his arm to Annaca. She smiled and accepted.

"So, where should we start? We could walk around or get food. Do you ride any of the rides?" Annaca asked.

"I can handle a ride or two. It's Lady's choice." Austin answered.

Annaca squealed like a kid, "My favorite ride is the tilt-a-whirl. I love to spin the car until it makes me feel like I'm part of the ride."

Austin shook his head and let out a hearty laugh. "The line doesn't look that long; let's grab some tickets and go for it!"

They walked arm and arm to the ticket booth and purchased a small fortune in tickets. As they walked around, they could see tired parents being pulled to different attractions by children pleading to do everything. There was a little boy waiting in line with his mom, catching snowflakes with his tongue.

The smell of fried food, funnel cakes, popcorn and emissions from the rides wafted in the cold air. It may have started out lonely for Annaca, but a change was initiated by a stranger who just had to meet her.

Austin escorted Annaca to the Tilt-a-Whirl. They waited in line for a moment. They walked arm and arm up the ramp, and Austin gestured for her to take the inside seat. Either spot would have been satisfactory to Annaca. Just being on the ride and giving up control to the gravitational force was well worth it.

It was just a moment to escape the world and to feel like a kid. It was a memory in time to feel carefree. She always loved the adrenaline rush she got on the ride.

The ride started, and a huge smile spread across Annaca's face. Austin looked over and saw her smile. He wanted to kiss her. She was beautiful, and he couldn't resist the temptation, so he leaned in to kiss her on the cheek. Annaca was surprised, but it was sweet. She touched her cheek as to savor the kiss.

"What was that for?" She asked.

"Sorry, I couldn't resist. You looked so happy and beautiful." He said.

Their car started to climb the hill and spin. They slid together in the center and held the bar tight. Giggling like children, the entire ride. Annaca couldn't contain her smile. It felt great to enjoy the festival without a care in the world. It was a brief moment of freedom from reality.

The ride came to a halt and they were beckoned to exit the ride. Another ride was needed, so they ran across the ramps to the exit. Austin smiled and offered up his hand to lead her on their next fleeting adventure ride. Fingers locked together, they were skipping to the scrambler. It was a ride of spinning and gravity. They waited their turn in line.

He let her take the inside so she would squish him each time the ride extended out. Annaca grinned and apologized each time she slammed into him. He didn't care. He extended his arm out and wrapped it around her to pull her in tight so the impact was only on one side. Annaca welcomed the embrace. It was a wonderful feeling.

It was a good thing it was cold during this time. If not, she wouldn't have been able to keep bugs out of her teeth because she couldn't stop smiling. This was the most fun she has had in forever. She was having an actual pleasurable time without sexual interaction. The fact that he wasn't trying to drag her off to a dark corner purely for sex made her want him even more. It was intriguing that he was innocently sweet.

Laughter and screams of joy floated all through the air of the festival. The ride had finished, and they exited onto the ramps. Standing in the middle of the walkway, they looked around trying to decide what to do next. Austin grinned at Annaca as he swiped a chunk of hair out of her face and tucked it behind her ear. Annaca was startled, though it was a sweet gesture. She waited to see if he would try to steal another kiss, but he looked away.

"Are you hungry?" He asked.

She shrugged her shoulders and said, "I could go for a funnel cake."

"Well then, we need some funnel cake." Austin said.

He extended his hand for her to take. She accepted, and they sauntered over to the nearest fried food seller. They stood in line, arm and arm, talking about what ride they should try next. Annaca had a different plan in mind, though.

She wanted to ride him. She wanted to take him out for a test drive. His innocent ways were driving her crazy, and her desire was burning through her body.

It was their turn to order. Austin stepped up and purchased a funnel cake and a soda to wash it down.

"Hope you don't mind, I figured we could share." He said with a wink.

Annaca blushed a bit because her mind was not on food or soda. She was sizing him up while he ordered and got caught with her eyes checking his package. Filled with embarrassment, she glanced away. Despite being caught, she was more excited to ride him next. She just hoped that the package she saw was worth the trouble.

"Were you just checking me out?" Austin asked with a naughty twinkle in his eye.

"Well, if I say yes, would you be mad?" Annaca asked.

Austin laughed and shook his head. "Darlin', I have been wondering all night if you were even interested in someone like me."

Distracted, though happy with his statement, Annaca grinned and moved in to kiss him. He grinned at her and reached for her face. His warm hands caressed her jaw as he gently kissed her lips. The heat of his breath against her lips sent a slight shiver down her spine. This kiss was different. It was more genuine than any other kiss she had ever felt. She couldn't explain it.

The sensation was a firework display in her mind. Weston was no longer a thought in her mind. This man provoked her lust with just one kiss. Annaca never thought that would be possible. The energy was fleeting with others, but this one had her attention. Annaca didn't care that they were downtown. She didn't care that hundreds of people were walking by. She wanted him right there, right now. He was gorgeous in his own country way. She couldn't control her lustful thoughts.

Pulling out of the kiss, Austin looked deep into her eyes with a gentle grin. "Ms. Annaca, I really enjoy kissing you, but we should stop. I have a lot going on, and I really can't do this right now. It's not that I don't desire you. I just don't want to give you the wrong impression of me."

Shocked, Annaca replied, "But you just asked if I found you attractive. I am really confused."

"Well, it's my job. I don't want you to think differently of me when you find out what I do." Austin answered.

"Well, it's not like we are dating, so why would I think differently of you? I'm pretty open-minded. I'm just looking to spend some time with someone like you," Annaca smoothly replied.

Austin wasn't sure how to take her statement other than to ask, "So, are you just looking for sex and occasional company?"

"Is there anything wrong with that?" Annaca asked.

"I'm a bit surprised; there are not many girls who don't want a commitment of some sort." Austin answered.

"With that figured out, what is this profession that you are so worried about?" Annaca asked.

Austin blushed a bit and rubbed the back of his neck with his hand. "Well, I uh, I'm a stripper at a local nightclub here in town. I make decent money at it. I'm super shy, though. The thing is, I'm a different person at work."

Annaca smiled and reached for his face, cupping his cheeks in her hands. "I have no idea how you could be shy with that type of job, but I promise, I won't hold it against you."

She pulled his face to hers and kissed his lips softly.

Austin smiled sweetly and asked, "So what would you like to do now?"

Annaca grinned and said, "Well, I do have one thing in mind, but that is if you are up for it."

Austin's face fell. "I was kind of hoping for festival rides or something to do with the festival. I rarely get the chance to just be a normal person instead of a piece of meat for women... sometimes men, it's weird."

Annaca pouted and replied. "Well, we can go on some more rides or play a couple of the carnival games. To be honest, I don't get to be a kid much either, and this is a delightful change."

They stared into each other's eyes for a moment or two and made the choice to hit up a couple more rides. Moments later, they were back to laughing and giggling like the children running around the festival. They found one of those games where you can win a fish by throwing a ring around a bottle. Annaca tried first, and she missed all of them.

Austin grinned at her and said, "Let me try. I will win you a fish." His first two whizzed through the bottles and missed. He focused on the third ring, flicked his wrist like he was skipping a stone across the water and a buzzer sounded.

"Woo hoo!! See, I told you I would win you a fish." Austin smirked.

The game attendant told him to pick out his fish. Annaca pointed to the little white and orange fish swimming around in its bag. The game operator handed the fish to Annaca. She smiled so wide holding this little creature in her hands.

Austin peered into the bag and asked, "So what are you going to name it?"

Annaca marveled at the little one flicking around and thought for a moment. "Hmmm, I think I will call him Jack. He can be my main man. I can read to him, and we will just hang out in my flat. He's perfect. Thank you for my new buddy."

Austin looked into the bag and said, "Alight Jack, you make sure you keep Ms. Annaca company. Well, we are going to have to find a tank for him and food along with all the neat little plastic plants to give him stuff to swim around."

Annaca didn't know what to think. She hasn't had a pet for a long time. It was a good thing that she didn't have to walk him or anything. She was filled with a warm, fuzzy feeling to have a little guy to talk to that wouldn't give her a hard time.

Time flew by, and it was ten minutes to midnight on New Year's Eve. Austin and Annaca proceeded to the center of the festival, where a huge clock tower stood. All the patrons of the festival had gathered around the clock to celebrate and ring in the New Year. Snow flurries were flying all around the crowd.

Couples were snuggled up to fight the chill in the air. Positive vibes were all around despite the cold. Annaca stuffed Jack into her inside pocket to keep him warm.

It was now thirty seconds to midnight, and the crowd started to chant. "30, 29, 28..." Austin offered his hand to Annaca. She accepted, and he pulled her closer. He stared deep into her eyes and grinned as he started counting with the rest of the crowd. Annaca grinned and joined in the counting, "10, 9, 8...."

The clock struck midnight, and the chimes rang out. Austin leaned in and kissed Annaca sweetly.

"Happy New Year! I hope you have the best year yet." Austin said.

Annaca smirked up at him and tried to kiss him one more time, but he pulled away. Annaca was confused, but tried to stay happy. She turned to cheer with the crowd and watch everyone join in the singing and dancing around the clock. The atmosphere was filled with hopeful wishes for a better year.

Annaca turned back around to face Austin, but he was nowhere to be found. Frantic, she searched the crowd to see if he had gone to get food or a drink or something. He had kissed her and disappeared into thin air. She was uneasy. Feeling like she was dropped like a bad habit.

She walked away from the crowd and started to head home. She just didn't understand. What did she do wrong? Her holiday spirit was ripped away, just like that. The only comfort she had was her new little guy. Tomorrow she would go to town and get all the stuff he needed.

When she got home from the festival, she changed into a pair of warm, fuzzy flannel pajamas. Thoughts swirled around in her head about the evening events. She just wanted to go to sleep, but she couldn't. She was flustered with the fact that another man had just left her hanging without a word.

She grabbed one of her favorite books off the bedside table and climbed into bed. Jack swam around in his bag on her nightstand. All propped up with pillows and a warm comforter, she opened her book and began to read.

"Once upon a time there was a princess who wanted to be common. She longed to escape the trials and tribulations of royal life. This princess was overwhelmed with the responsibilities of training to be queen. *She was a daydreamer* who *longed for adventure and the pleasures of a simple life. The queen constantly had a guard watch the princess because the princess had become a clever escape artist....."*

Annaca started to drift off to sleep, dreaming about being a wayward princess who longed for adventure. When she awoke the next morning, the book was still clutched in her hand. Even though the evening before had sucked at the end, she told herself that this New Year was going to be better. She poked the bag and told Jack, "Good morning, my little love. At least you won't leave me."

She got up and made her usual cup of coffee and climbed back into bed and snuggled back in. She sipped her coffee and picked her book back up. Sunday was a day for relaxing. She was going to drink coffee and read to Jack.

"Jack, oh shit, I have to go to town and get you a tank." Annaca groaned.

She put her book down, chugged her coffee and got dressed for the day. She could get a tank and supplies for him quickly and get back to being a snuggled up bookworm.

Chapter Twelve

Ryder's

She had only seen him at the festival for a short while, but it was exhilarating. His simple smile was sweet and teasing. He only advanced for a kiss. He hadn't pushed any further for anything. Annaca pushed for so much more, though. She couldn't get it out of her head.

Annaca wanted to see him again and take advantage of his simple, countrified body. She was not used to being told "No" in any way. She was completely perplexed. This hurt more than when Weston disappeared on her. All she had was Jack as a reminder of her evening. Jack had already become her everything.

She spent hours watching him swim around in his new home. His tank was meant for a beta fish, but he had neon green rocks with colorful plants to swim through. She found a cute little bubbling pirate chest with a diver that was an adorable addition to his little home. Jack loved his little tank. It was definitely bigger than the bag that he was brought home in.

Annaca couldn't escape the thoughts of Austin despite how much she watched Jack. She wanted to run her hands through his curly hair as he was kissing her neck with gentle nibbles. The thought of his warm breath against her skin gave her chills. She could feel his fingers sliding down her side and across her waistline. Begging for his hand to move south and tease her body.

She wanted more than just his hands all over her body. Thinking about it, she knew what he did for work. Acting on her decision, she looked up all the male strip clubs in town. Her search turned up with two results; Ryder's and another one on the outskirts of town called Charmers. She felt like a stalker.

Yet, her curiosity about this man, who had just disappeared, was an uplifting distraction from her day-to-day life. She wondered how he would react if she just showed up at one of his shows, sitting in the front row. She let her mind wander through their encounter.

As always, Annaca's imagination was running wild. Even though he left her on the spot, she wondered what it would be like; she'd never been to a live strip show. Of course, she'd seen brief clips and videos on the internet. But she had never attended a live strip show with hot guys dancing around and provocatively removing clothing. Since she couldn't get Austin out of her head, she decided to call Carlene to make plans.

"Hey girl, I got a story and a question for you. First, how do you feel about going to a strip show?" Annaca asked.

Carlene had never been to a strip club either, so it sounded like a girl's night out in the making.

"What could it hurt? Drunk women staring at half-naked men and screaming as they take their clothes off? Sounds like a blast!" Carlene exclaimed.

Annaca explained the events that took place during the festival on New Year's Eve. With disappointment in her tone, Annaca described the entire episode. She sent Carlene a picture of Jack.

"Aww, he's adorable. Look at his little tank." Carlene squealed.

"That does seem peculiar that he would just disappear like that. From what you said, it sounds like he was hiding another woman or something. You did nothing wrong. Or, maybe he's just really shy," Carlene explained.

"I just don't understand it. Never has a guy just disappeared like that. I mean, except, Weston. Hopefully, when we find his show and attend, he won't be upset by it." Annaca sighed.

"Well, if he gets mad, he isn't worth your time, love. It's not like you're in love with him or anything.... Are you?" Carlene inquired.

"Oh, no, not in love, I am definitely in lust though. His muscular definition was cloaked under all those clothes. His ass looked great in those tight jeans, and I just wanted to save the horse and fuck the cowboy." Annaca snickered.

"Well, since he said *in town*, I can only assume that he was referring to Ryder's. So, Friday night, you and me, we are going to drool over some men. We should probably bring some napkins with us. And, don't forget your dollar bills!" Annaca squealed.

"Okay, sounds like a plan, and we are in for one hell of a ladies' night out!" Carlene said cheerfully.

"Yes, we are! I know I'm looking for one specifically, but there will be plenty of eye candy. Anyways, I'll talk to you later. Love you, girl," Annaca said.

"Sounds like a great time. Love you too. Bye, girl." Carlene replied.

Annaca started searching through all the club's pictures on the website to see if there was any indication that Austin worked there. The fact that he turned her down and then disappeared was throwing her for a loop. She couldn't get him out of her mind, and it was driving her crazy. It was difficult to rein in her curiosity about why he would be ashamed of his profession.

She was sitting on her chaise lounge with a blue flannel blanket covering her long legs. Scrolling through pictures, Annaca thought she had seen Austin. The pictures made it difficult to tell because his face was completely covered with a red paisley bandanna. She zoomed in on a particular picture, and she saw his eyes. She knew it.

His piercing blue eyes caught her attention. She started searching for Friday to make sure he would be there. She was in luck; they had a new show premiering Friday; with six gorgeous men in a two-hour, choreographed show. The website said that the show started at eight o'clock. *Perfect*, she thought.

She grabbed her cell phone and immediately sent a text to Carlene. "Girl, get your drool cloth and dollar bills, the show starts at eight on Friday!!!"

Carlene heard her phone and picked it up off the table. Reading through Annaca's message, she shook her head because she knew this was going to be crazy. Annaca is a wild child and a riot to be around. She could raise a lot of hell when she felt like causing some trouble. Carlene knew this was going to be fun.

The week seemed to drag by for Annaca. She kept busy with her work and maintained her sales record at the company. She just wanted to see the look on his face when she walked into the club and sat in the front row by the stage. Maybe she was a little obsessed, but she had never been evaded by a man before, and she wanted a petty revenge of sorts.

Two hours before the show and she was blowing up Carlene's phone with excitement. Annaca could barely contain herself. It was her first real strip show, and she couldn't wait.

Carlene was rushing to go pick her up so they could get this over with. They were both nervous, not knowing what to expect with a show like this.

One hour left, and both girls were at Annaca's flat doing final touches on makeup and double checking their outfits. They wanted to look perfect before they walked out that door. Annaca switched between four different outfits, before she finally decided on a sleek black dress with a slit up to her hip and a plunging cut in the bust line.

She was gorgeous as always. Crimson lips grinned into the mirror as Annaca brushed her long ebony hair one last time. She wanted tonight to be special, with a twist of planned fate.

Prepped for the night and ready to watch men dance around for their entertainment, the girls grabbed their stuff and walked out the door and descended the stairs from the flat.

Two amazing women were about to prey on a group of unsuspecting men. The girls exited the bottom entrance of the flat and walked to the sidewalk. They stood there for a few moments trying to get the attention of a cab. Carlene hailed one to stop. They climbed in and told the driver to take them to Ryder's.

Without further delay, they were on their way. Ten minutes later, they were in front of Ryder's. Neon lights were all over the building, and ecstatic women were all in line to get into the club. The sign read, "Country Eye Candy".

The girls scurried out of the cab and rushed to get in line before it got overwhelming. All along the line, women were excitedly chatting. There was one woman who was super obnoxious. Her laugh was twice as bad. She sounded like a scalded dog. Carlene and Annaca glanced at each other when the woman laughed, and they tried to conceal their snickering.

"I hope the music is loud." Carlene sneered.

Annaca nodded in agreement. As the girls moved up the line, they could feel the pounding bass vibrating their feet. Their excitement grew each time the line moved up. The atmosphere was saturated with sexual tension energy from all the horny women. It was like watching a group of overexuberant children jostling in line to the giant playground of their dreams.

The bouncer at the door stood six foot four easily. He wore a black felt cowboy hat with a pearly white grin, a black leather vest that exposed rippling arm muscles and a pair of tight Wrangler blue jeans that were accented by black snakeskin boots. He was checking IDs and stamping hands with a blue "X". Carlene nudged Annaca, hinting toward the bouncer. Annaca grinned and shook her head. She had one man on her mind, and she was praying he was inside.

Carlene flashed a sheepish grin at the bouncer while he stamped her hand.

The bouncer winked at her and said, "You ladies have a wonderful night. I'm available for a private show later."

They giggled and dashed inside. The music was a mix of hip hop, rock, country and booty dance. The DJ was in a corner booth, bouncing around with each mix that she made. Headphones hung around her neck. She was a cute little blond with bright red lips and a pink and purple tie-dyed tank-top.

Her jewelry was simple; she wore bangle bracelets and a silver Figaro necklace that bounced off her cleavage every time she moved. She had her long straight blond hair pulled into a black baseball cap with the club logo. She was quite energetic, and her music flowed well. Everyone listened to her because she announced when the men went on stage.

A colorful display of lights was flashing all over the club. There were rustic chairs and tables on the concrete floor that surrounded the wooden dance floor. Country styled art and decorations covered the walls. The bartenders were all males in vests, jeans and boots topped with a cowboy hat.

What a wonderful thing, a country club in the middle of town. Annaca marveled at the establishment while she was searching for Austin. Despite the nervous feeling in the pit of her stomach, she wanted to catch his eye.

The DJ announced that the show started in ten minutes and suggested that everyone grab a seat. Annaca grabbed Carlene and hooked her arm to drag her to the front of the stage. A few rows of chairs were in front of the stage. Annaca sat dead center, and Carlene sat to the right of her.

One dancer walked out from behind the DJ booth and onto the stage with a microphone. He had on a tan straw cowboy hat, a multicolored flannel with the sleeves ripped off, a pair of tight Wrangler jeans, and a brown belt with a golden horseshoe buckle. He was all muscle and had a gorgeous smile that would make any girl cream her panties.

All the women started hollering and cheering for the men. The room was hormonally charged with women waiting to tuck dollar bills into g-strings.

The cowboy on stage introduced himself and explained a bit of how the show was going to go. The women cheered every time he stopped talking. As he finished his introduction, five other men, dressed about the same, filtered onto the stage. They took their positions on stage, and the lead man cued the DJ to start the music.

Annaca watched as the men started their show, and then she saw him; to the left of the stage was Austin. He was dressed identically to the lead man, and everything about his body was unbelievable. *How did she not see it at the festival?* Rippling muscles flexed as he danced. Sweat beaded up on all the men from moving while the stage lights heated them up.

Annaca got a rush of excitement waiting for him to recognize her. For a glimpse of a second, he saw her. A wave of panic flashed across his face for a moment, and then his game face was right back with a huge smile as he directed his attention to the major crowd.

Annaca grinned to herself because she knew he saw her, and she made him nervous. She watched the show with Carlene, and they both hooted and hollered as the guys danced around stripping away what little clothing they had on. Annaca couldn't take her eyes off of Austin. She watched him strip his shirt off; displaying his rippling pectorals. He didn't have a chiseled body, but he was physically fit and his muscle definition was on point. Annaca watched as his arm muscles bulged. The sweat on his body was glistening in the light.

She kept getting a twinge of horny excitement with every move she watched. She desperately wanted to ride this cowboy all night long. Annaca was dancing and grinding in her seat with the music. Her hormones were on fire. It was riveting to watch the guys. Not a single pair of panties was dry in the room.

The guy in a black cowboy hat and a royal blue g-string pulled a lady onto the stage. She had to be at least fifty, but she looked great for her age. She was athletically built, with auburn colored hair, a cute little ass, crystal blue eyes and a grin a mile wide.

Her face turned as red as her fiery hair when all the guys circled her while grinding on her. There was a tall, extremely built man who got down on his knees and put his face in the redhead's lap. He shot straight up and then pulled her face into his G-string. The women in the crowd were going wild, screaming, yelling and waving cash in the air hoping for their turn.

Carlene was having a blast watching the show. She kept nudging Annaca and pointing out different things that the guys were doing. Austin caught sight of Carlene and chose her as his next target. It was his job after all. Dancing and clapping his hands to the music, he sauntered his way to Carlene. Once Carlene realized he was targeting her, she stood up and started waving her fistful of ones as high as she could.

Austin motioned for another guy to come over and dance around Carlene. Austin grinned at her and used his hands to rub up and down her sides as he danced in front of her. He leaned back and pulled the side of his deep purple g-string out for Carlene to put dollars in. Carlene obliged with a flirtatious smile.

Annaca was mildly jealous as her hand shot up into the air; displaying her cash looking for a g-string. She really wanted Austin, but it seemed he was trying to ignore her. *Two can play this game*, she thought. The man with a candy apple red g-string and a dark brown cowboy hat moved in. He played with Annaca's hair and moved his hands down to her shoulders. Because her cleavage was proud and prominent, his fingers outlined her dress from cleavage to her sides, continuing to her slit on her thigh.

A shiver of hormonal surges went through her whole body. She could take any of these guys right there on the stage, in front of everyone. She was so sexually charged and frustrated, she couldn't care less. The more he touched her, the more she shook with pleasurable vibrations. She tried to put her hands on him, but he removed them and shook his finger at her.

She pouted and looked over at Austin. Austin caught her glance and decided he had teased her long enough. He motioned for the other guy to switch women. Annaca cheese grinned as Austin danced his way to her. Annaca immediately slid a twenty into the front of his g-string trying to get an idea of what he had to offer.

He smiled at her but looked apprehensive as she did it. After slipping the twenty into his g-string, she moved her hands to his hips and held on while he danced in front of her.

He leaned in and whispered into her ear, "Well, you found me, now what are you going to do with me?"

Annaca smirked and replied, "You will never know unless we can go somewhere more private. Don't get me wrong, I would take you right here on this stage, in front of everyone without a second thought."

Austin was speechless. He was used to little old ladies being handsy. The guys rarely entertained young women.

Annaca smiled and answered, "You, I hope."

Austin leaned in and whispered in her ear, "Wait for me after the show? I'll give you that ride you have been waiting for."

He leaned back and winked at her as he moved in to another group of women flashing handfuls of dollars.

Annaca's grin grew across her face. She couldn't wait to get hold of him. She just had a feeling that he would be a ride worth waiting for.

Carlene was having a blast. She was slowly losing her voice from screaming and hollering at the guys. Annaca and her danced through the night. One guy in particular had caught her attention.

She nudged Annaca and asked, "Do you think Austin could put in a word for me with that one?"

She pointed to a tall and bronzed man with a shiny green g-string and a black cowboy hat.

Annaca laughed and said, "I will see what I can do."

The show went on for about another half hour. The women patrons were drunk and falling chaotically around the establishment. Their voices were hoarse from screaming all night long. The guys seemed to be worn out. It was a wonderful first show for Annaca and Carlene.

The DJ called for last call and suggested that everyone didn't have to go home, but they couldn't stay in the bar. There was a loud "awww" across the bar, but the crowd was exhausted. They lined up to pay their tabs and head out the door.

Annaca and Carlene walked out the door and sat to the left of the building, hoping to catch two gorgeous guys walking out. Annaca mentally prepared herself. She hoped for the best, but she composed herself for the worst probable outcome.

A few drunken women stumbled out of the club laughing and carrying on about the show. Annaca looked up and laughed as the women worked their way to their cars and ways home. A few minutes later, the staff of the bar filtered out. Annaca and Carlene watched the door for Austin and his friends. Austin poked his head out the door to check to see if she was still there. The guy whom Carlene has asked about was right behind him.

The guys were back in street attire. They stepped out and smiled at the girls.

Austin gestured to his friend, talking to Carlene. "This is Trevor. If you are interested, he will escort you home."

Carlene's face lit up, and she nodded her head rapidly. Trevor stepped toward Carlene and offered his arm as they both hailed a cab to her place. Carlene gave Annaca a huge grin and a wave as the cab pulled up. Annaca gave a little wave to say congratulations. She was happy that her friend was going to get some attention from a man. She deserved it since she had been hearing all of Annaca's little adventures.

Austin stepped closer to Annaca and asked, "So, you got to see everything. Still want something to do with me?"

Annaca stood up and smiled back at him. "Of course. Watching what you can do with that body of yours, I want you even more. The show was impressive, by the way. It was my first encounter with exotic dancers."

Austin blushed and said, "I'm glad you liked it. Didn't really want you to see it, but I hope it doesn't change your opinion of me."

Annaca looked a bit puzzled and asked, "Why would I see you any differently? You are a gorgeous man, you are super sweet, and I had a blast at the festival until you took off on me... You owe me big time now."

Austin hung his head and scratched the back of his neck as he said, "Yeah, I'm really sorry about that. I didn't want to give you the wrong impression, and I wasn't sure I could go through with anything since we were both stood up. I felt I deserved an explanation before I tried to move on with you."

Annaca used her fingertips to pull his chin up, "I completely understand. Now, since you are free to roam, would you like to go somewhere, or do you want to stay out here all night?"

Austin smirked and said, "Well, we could go back to your place or, if you are up for it, my truck is out back and we could go for a ride."

Annaca's face lit up as she exclaimed, "I would love that. I haven't been able to go for a ride in forever. Maybe we can find a road out of the city and see some stars?"

Austin nodded and offered his arm to Annaca as he escorted her to his truck parked behind the club. Annaca's face had a wide, toothy grin plastered on, and she couldn't contain her excitement. She was ready for a country drive and a midnight ride on a cowboy.

Chapter Thirteen

Country Night

Austin walked Annaca to the passenger side of his truck. He unlocked the door and opened it so she could climb in. She smiled at him as he closed the door. He hurried around the back of the truck to the driver's side. Annaca stretched across the seat to unlock his door. He climbed in and dug in his pocket searching for his keys.

He pulled out the keys to an old red '87 Chevy. He cranked it up with a rumble and grinned at Annaca. She smiled back at him and asked if he could turn up the heat. As Annaca shivered from the chill of the night air, Austin reached behind him and pulled out a dark blue heavy jacket to offer her.

"It will take a minute for the truck to warm up; I hope this will help until then." He said with a smirk.

Annaca accepted the jacket and wrapped up in it. Austin backed out of the parking spot and headed out onto the street. He got to the traffic light and hung a right toward the outside of the city. He switched on his old radio to a country music station but left the volume down enough so they could talk.

Annaca quietly sang along to a song she remembered most of the words to, and Austin just grinned as he watched her. There was something about the way she could be so innocent. He was enchanted by her. She was passive yet aggressive. He could see more of her countryside the further away from the city they got.

Annaca was ready to see an open starlit sky without the orange hue of city lights. The kid in her was trying to show through, and she didn't care. The country boy next to her aroused the woman inside. Anticipation welled up inside of her as he decided on a location to pull over to. She looked over at Austin as she placed her hand on his knee, waiting for him to push her away, but he didn't.

He just smiled and shook his head. Annaca waited a moment, and then she caressed his leg just above his knee. She felt his leg muscles tense up. Instead of stopping her, Austin placed his hand on hers and pulled her hand to the top of his thigh. Annaca grinned and continued to rub the inside of his right thigh.

She felt his pants rise just above her hand. Annaca smirked because she knew she was going to get what she wanted from him. Austin pulled into an open field. He looked at her as he kicked the truck sideways to show off a bit. He drove to the middle of the field, where the sky was a brilliant display of stars shining in the indigo darkness.

Austin stopped and put the truck into park. He left it running because it was so cold. The Chevy purred quietly under them. Annaca got a shiver of excitement; she was ready to enjoy this little adventure.

Austin, being a country boy that was always prepared, asked, "Would you like a beer out of the cooler? And I have blankets in my toolbox if you would like to see the stars more clearly."

Annaca blushed a bit and replied, "That sounds wonderful."

Austin grinned and said, "How about you stay here in the heat and I'll set everything up real quick."

Annaca nodded and pulled the jacket tighter around her.

Austin hopped out of the truck and rummaged around in the back, making all kinds of noise. He shook out a couple of blankets and laid them down in the bed of the truck. He even pulled a couple of pillows out of his toolbox. Annaca laughed to herself about all the fuss he was making.

I wonder what else he has stashed in that toolbox. Or how many times has he done this before? She thought.

Austin hopped out of the bed of the truck and opened the driver's side door. He shut the truck off, closed his door and went around to her side. He opened the door and offered her his hand. She accepted and hopped down. She smiled up at him, and he grinned back at her. He leaned in and kissed her slowly. Annaca welcomed the kiss as he wrapped his arms around her, trying to keep her warm.

He pulled back from the kiss and just watched her. She was simply beautiful. Women threw themselves at him all the time at his job, but this one wanted him before she knew about his job.

Austin smiled and asked, "Would you like to get in the bed so you can cover up? I put a couple of pillows back there too."

Annaca nodded as she shivered. Austin reached past her and got two beer koozies out of his glove box.

"I figure we will need these. We need to keep your hands warm." Austin grinned.

Annaca smirked at him, shook her head, as she waited for him to lead the way to the truck bed.

Austin walked her to the back of the truck as he offered his arm so she could clamber up into the truck bed. She crawled toward the front of the truck and hurried to get under the blankets. Austin followed her and got under the covers as well. He kicked back with one arm behind his head and the other stretched out for Annaca to curl up into.

She welcomed his body heat since she was in a skimpy dress that wasn't made for the cooler country night air. Austin pulled her in tight to his side and gazed up at the stars. Annaca grinned as she laid her head in the crook of his arm, gazing into the night sky. The stars and the brilliance of the moon mesmerized her.

Though it was cold, it was a perfect country night. She was finally with the man who was just on stage in a g-string, dancing for a bunch of screaming women. Annaca enjoyed the embrace, but she had other plans in store for Austin. She wanted to ride this country boy in the bed of his old Chevy. She saw his performance, and now it was time to show him her skills.

Feeling restless, Annaca grazed her hand up and down his chest. She wanted to continue where they had left off. Expecting him to keep his promise, she was ready for that midnight country boy ride.

Austin seemed to get the hint quickly. His hand, which had wrapped around her shoulder, ventured down her arm and on down to caress her hip. He paused at her hip for a moment and then his hand grazed her tight little ass as if he was checking out the merchandise. Annaca didn't mind at all. She picked her head up with amusement.

Slowly, she sat up and moved in for a kiss. He didn't fight her or act shy at all. He leaned in and kissed her, just as he had kissed her the first time. Annaca caressed his cheek with her hand as she pressed her lips into his. Austin cracked his mouth, and he licked her bottom lip. Surprised, Annaca leaned back and looked at him.

She beamed down at him because she kind of liked it. Annaca leaned back in to kiss him, and he gently sucked on her bottom lip. It was simply enticing. Annaca decided she was going to control the situation since he was being playful. She wanted to play a little harder.

She climbed on top of him and mounted him. She shivered as the blanket slipped off her back. When she shivered, she wiggled her hips. She could feel him poke her between her thighs through his tight jeans. Annaca smirked as she gripped him with her thighs. Her cold fingertips slipped under his shirt as she ran her hands up his firm chest. He cracked a smile up at her as he shuddered from her icy touch.

He grabbed onto her hips as he encouraged her to grind on top of him. Annaca obliged with gyrations of her hips. She reached for his hands and pulled them to the inside of her thighs. He responded the way she had hoped as he pulled at her panties. Gently, he tugged at them again. He wanted deep inside her just as much as she wanted to ride him.

Annaca stood straight up. Austin reached up with both hands and pulled her lacy ruby red panties to her ankles. Annaca stepped out of them, and he threw them to the side. She lowered herself down to where she could sit in his lap again. Before she got all the way down, he slid down to where she would position herself on his face.

Annaca loved the idea of what he was intending to do. Spreading her knees further apart, she grabbed both his muscular arms. Raising his arms above his head, and pinned them down as she leaned forward. She could feel the heat of his breath on her core as she prepared for the flickering of his tongue.

The stubble on his face tickled the inside of her thighs. Annaca flinched with each stroke of his tongue. She could feel him trace a zigzag pattern as she gripped his arms tighter. Her hips rocked to increase the intensity of his lick. Austin kept trying to pull his arms out of Annaca's grasp. He wanted to grip her ass and pull her in tighter.

She tasted sweet. He gently sucked her clit, and she let out a groan. She was getting close, as her juices moistened his face. Austin finally broke free of her grasp. He slapped her ass cheeks as he pulled her in. Annaca's hands smacked against the back glass of the truck as she squealed with climax. She was in lust with this man's mouth. Austin had a cheesy grin on his face as he used his sleeve as a napkin.

Shaking, Annaca lifted herself up, so Austin could slide up. Annaca stayed propped up as best she could demanding that he take his pants off right then. He unbuckled his belt, unzipped his jeans and slid them down to his knees. Annaca grinned at him as she watched his rock hard cock spring free of his jeans.

Austin was already standing at attention, but she wanted to tease him a bit. She ran her fingers up and down his shaft. Each time she reached the head, she would swirl her fingers around it and gently pinch it. She leaned down and took him into her mouth, running her tongue down his length. She pulled back, trying not to get him too excited.

Austin was more than ready to feel her from the inside. Being cheesy, he joked about being ready to check her temperature.

Annaca snickered and said, "Alright. Tell me if I'm hot enough for you." She steadied herself to slide on to his pole.

Austin grabbed her hips and slowly positioned her. Annaca spread her knees out again and eased her way down. As he slid in, her juices lubricated his slide into home base. They moaned simultaneously from the sensation. Their cries of pleasure echoed into the night sky.

He caressed her ass while she slid up and down his throbbing cock. Her skin was smooth to the touch. He grabbed her hips and started thrusting up each time she would slow down. Their rhythm was sporadic, but that didn't stop them.

Occasionally, she stopped at the top with mini quick bounces, causing his tip to just barely penetrate inside. Austin would try to thrust up, but Annaca would stop him each time.

As she rocked back and forth, he matched her rhythm. Bliss was moments away. She grinned down at him as he intensified his thrust by lifting his hips. He was seconds away from getting off. Suddenly, he stopped her.

Austin sat up with Annaca in his lap. He leaned in for a kiss, and she gladly returned it. She was bewildered at first until he scooped her up and got up on his knees. In a flash, he switched positions with her. He looked down at her and winked. Carefully, he laid her back and grabbed both of her ankles, placing one on each of his shoulders. Annaca was astonished, but she let him take control.

He scooted up under her with his knees, to angle her upward. Annaca knew what was coming, so she placed her hands behind her head to brace herself against the bed of the truck. She didn't need a concussion from her head slamming into the bed wall. He inched his way up enough to glide into her. He held onto her thighs as he worked his way into her steamy sweet spot.

She was already wet from before, but the penetration of this angle felt like a heated explosion. Her moan was high pitched and echoed off the distant trees. The sound seemed to make Austin's cock swell more. His thrusts were forceful, but nothing Annaca couldn't handle. Annaca begged him to work faster. He perfectly hit her G-spot from this position. Her body was vibrating with another climax about to hit.

She wasn't able to grip anything with her hands, even though she wanted to dig into him and hold on tight. He kissed up and down her right leg as he continued to pleasure both of them. His cock was throbbing inside of her, and it wouldn't be long before he climaxed. Annaca squeezed all her muscles tight, hoping to finish before he did.

She arched her back and grasped the backs of his thighs. As she did that, he hit home. Her body tensed up. They both started shaking from coming so hard. It was so good she could see rainbow colors flashing behind her eyelids. She squirted fluid everywhere. Her mental state had collapsed. That sensation had never happened to her before.

Austin continued to pump into her tightened yet saturated loins. He trembled with each thrust. Annaca tightened every muscle, and he was defenseless against her sexual magic. Austin quivered. They gave it everything, and it was worth every second of waiting. Austin collapsed on top of Annaca.

Their bodies were tense and covered in sweat despite the chilly night air. They needed to relax their tight muscles after that workout. They released their grip on each other, extended their legs and stretched. His head rested on her left shoulder. They both inhaled deeply, trying to catch their breath. She rubbed his back, which was covered in sweat, and kissed his shoulder, gently working her way to his neck and then finding his lips.

Neither one had a care in the world. An icy breeze went across the bed of the truck, and they both shivered. Annaca grasped at the blanket to pull it back over them. Austin snickered at her struggle. He helped pull the blanket over them as he stared at her for a moment. He swept her hair away from her face, put his hand behind her neck and pulled her into a passionate, sweaty kiss. Annaca grazed his cheek with her soft hand as she slid her fingers into his hair.

Daylight was cresting over the horizon, and it was time to get going. They snuggled together for a moment before they gathered their clothing and possessions so they could head back to the city. Disappointed that their time was limited, yet satisfied for the moment.

Austin jumped down from the tailgate of his truck. He put his hand out so Annaca could hop down, then he walked her to the passenger side of the truck and opened the door for her. He kissed her and smacked her ass as she turned to hop up into the seat. Once she was in, he closed the door and ran around to the driver's side.

Like a kid full of energy, he started the truck up and let it warm up a bit before heading to the city. They talked a bit during the ride back to town, already making plans to hook up again. Acting like teenagers returning from a night of mischief.

Austin flicked on the running lights and offered for Annaca to slide closer to him. He grinned at her and put his arm around her to pull her in tight. He pulled out onto the highway that led back to reality. The drive seemed quicker than before.

They made it back to town. Austin pulled up in front of the old theater. He asked a few questions about it and seemed genuinely interested in the history. Leaving the truck running, he put on the parking brake and shifted the truck into neutral. He hopped out so he could open her door. Annaca popped out and leaned against the truck, still wrapped up in his coat.

Austin pressed her against the truck as he kissed her. He already wanted to have her again. He whispered in her ear and asked her to call him when they could take another drive into the country. Annaca nodded. Austin offered his arm so he could escort her to her door.

Annaca kissed him one more time, handed over his jacket and smiled as she walked through her door.

"Thank you for a wonderful night," She blew a kiss at him through the door.

Austin smirked and replied, "You are welcome. Let's do it again soon."

Annaca shook her head, sauntered up her stairs and entered her flat. She was home and blissfully exhausted. It was a mind-blowing night of sex, but not meaningful. It was just sex. She walked over to Jack's tank, kissed her fingers and pressed them to the glass.

"Morning, little man." She said as she sprinkled some pellets into his tank.

She was freezing after the late night escapades. She went to put some warmer clothes on and crawl into her bed, where she slept until the late afternoon.

Chapter Fourteen

Girl Pleasure

She was asking about a scarf in the window display of the department store when Annaca saw her. Annaca sized this girl up from bottom to top. Legs for days, gorgeous long curly blond hair, with a perfect heart shaped ass and easily a C cup. She would make a perfect version of a typical guy's fantasy. Annaca couldn't take her eyes off of her.

This young woman had her complete attention. Annaca had a flash of binding this girl with the scarf that she inquired about and having her way with her body. Laying her down right there in the display window and stripping her down while kissing her perfect little body. Annaca desired this new girl, and she couldn't stop admiring her appearance.

After watching this girl like a creeper, Annaca walked up and introduced herself. "I'm sorry; I just had to come tell you that you are gorgeous. By the way, my name is Annaca."

The girl blushed and seemed a bit set back. She wasn't used to women hitting on her.

"Well, thank you. You're stunning as well. My name is Alexandria, but everyone calls me Zandria." She replied.

"It's wonderful to meet you, Zandria. I was wondering if you would ever like a get a drink with me and my best friend, Carlene. She and I go to Makko's on Friday nights. You are more than welcome to join us. The bartender Jamie is super hot, and it's fun to watch him work." Annaca offered.

Zandria smiled and replied, "Sounds like a good time. Sure, why not? I haven't been out on a girls' night in a while."

Annaca smiled and said, "Alright, well we can show you a good time. Sounds like you may need one. See you, Friday? We usually get there around nine-thirty."

Zandria nodded in agreement and went back to looking at the scarf she was about to purchase. Annaca couldn't help herself. She watched her walk away. Her heart-shaped ass rocked up and down as she walked away. She was cute, and Annaca wanted to walk right behind her and feel her cheeks as they bounced.

She made a mental note as she thought about her ass in a pair of tight blue jeans. Annaca grinned to herself and walked to a different part of the store. She was looking for a jaw-dropping dress. Something that was long, red and had slits up the sides. She had a new lipstick that she wanted to try out with a dress that would get a yes from anyone she wanted.

After searching through a few dress racks, she found the perfect dress. The dress had a slit up to the hip on the sides. It was burgundy in color with a silver thread design encasing pea-sized rhinestone gems. It was a backless halter top with a plunging V-cut in the bust. Annaca grinned to herself. She knew this dress was it.

She adored the idea of the attention that she would catch, not to mention that it would make her girls stand out proudly. Shoes she needed a pair of silver heels to go with it. After all, shoes are a girl's best friend.

Friday night came quickly. Annaca was ready to see Zandria again. Annaca hoped Zandria would be interested in some one-on-one time. Even though it was a friendly girls' night out, it usually meant that Annaca was on the prowl for a new target to tease and please. Annaca couldn't help the fact that she just wanted to play.

Annaca's eyes locked on Zandria as she walked through the doors of Makko's. She was mid-sentence with Carlene, as she went silent. Zandria was wearing a black suede miniskirt with a brilliant red halter top. Black open-toed ankle boots wrapped around Zandria's feet.

Her curly blonde hair was wrapped up in a messy bun to show off a tattoo of a blue and green butterfly sitting on a black dragon with golden eyes on her right shoulder. Zandria strutted over to the girls and smiled as she sat down next to Annaca.

The tattoo intrigued Annaca as she used it as a conversation starter. "Hey Ms. Beautiful, how are you tonight? That is a gorgeous tattoo you have there."

Zandria blushed a bit and said, "Thanks. It's one of my favorites. I have a few more; I love my tattoos. My ink therapist always hooks me up."

Annaca smiled as she introduced Zandria to Carlene and explained how they met. Carlene already knew how this was going to go with Annaca. Her friend liked her variety. Carlene had her guy, and she was happy with him.

Jamie was behind the bar serving drinks while people watching. It was a slow Friday for Makko's. The girls were watching Jamie as he was trying to be slick and toss glasses and liquor bottles in the air. He poured the girls a shot and told them "cheers". The girls all toasted to another weekend and their seductive bartender.

The night continued as Jamie goofed around behind the bar for the girls' entertainment. A few couples came in for dinner. They watched Jamie perform while they waited for their food. Jamie was putting on quite a show. The girls would giggle every time he would wink at them as he finished another drink trick. The audience at Makko's cheered Jamie on.

As one couple walked out, they tipped him for the show. He finished up his last drink trick with a row of shots lined up along the bar. The shots were the colors of the rainbow, and he offered all the customers to come up and take a shot. A few people walked up and took a shot while the rest of the crowd gathered and applauded his efforts. Jamie bowed to his audience and thanked them.

Annaca turned to Zandria and asked what her plans were after the bar closed down.

Zandria shrugged her shoulders and said, "I'm not sure why? What do you have in mind?"

Annaca grinned at her and replied, "Well, I was wondering if you would like to hang out at my place afterward. I'm just curious."

Zandria was feeling tipsy and thought about it for a second.

She leaned over and whispered into Annaca's ear, "I have never been with a girl, and I'm not sure what to do. I mean, I know what I like, but I haven't tried to please another woman. That is, if you are asking about what I think you are asking about."

Annaca smirked and said, "Don't worry. I will introduce you to a world you have been missing out on. You will be pleasantly surprised."

Zandria smiled sheepishly. "I barely know you yet; I believe you."

Annaca was pleased that she was about to take a cherry. She wanted to treat Zandria, but didn't want to scare her away, though. Annaca leaned over and asked if she drove to Makko's. Zandria nodded yet looked curious about why she asked.

Annaca smiled and said, "Well, my flat is just down the road from here. We don't want to be driving around drunk."

Annaca had a couple of ideas swirling around her head, and she wanted to try something out with Zandria. She decided it was time to pay her tab and take Zandria for a spin.

She leaned over and whispered into Zandria's ear, "Hey, you want to get out of here?"

Zandria grinned, finished her shot and shook her head yes. Annaca smirked in return as they cleared their tabs. Hugging Carlene's neck, Annaca promised she would call her tomorrow. Annaca looped her arm through Zandria's; they both waved at Jamie and Carlene and walked out through the double glass doors.

Zandria was nervous. She's had sex before, but not with a woman. Annaca was so forward that Zandria had a feeling she wouldn't have to do much at all. She stopped walking with Annaca and pulled her to a halt.

"Here's my truck. I'm not sure where you want to go, but I can drive us there." Zandria stated.

Annaca smiled sweetly. "We can stay right here and I can ease you into this. I promise to be gentle. We don't need to drive anywhere; your truck bench seat will do."

Zandria was curious, so she attempted a kiss. Annaca figured out what she was trying to do, so she advanced by pinning Zandria to her candy-apple red Dodge. She pressed her body against Zandria's and cupped her face with her hands. Annaca gently pressed her lips to Zandria's and carefully kissed her. Zandria enjoyed the sensation, and she hungered for more. Annaca was a wonderful kisser.

Lipstick smeared across both of their faces as they continued to make out, just outside to the left of Makko's. They both tasted like alcohol and bad decisions, but they couldn't stop. The alcohol induced euphoria had kicked in full force. As Zandria continued to kiss Annaca, she could feel electricity running through her body.

She was eager for more. She grabbed the back of Annaca's head and laced her fingers together, locking Annaca into this kiss. Annaca's hands travelled up and down Zandria's body. She wanted to feel the trouble she was getting into. Zandria didn't even flinch at her warm touch; she encouraged it.

Annaca stopped her for a second and said, "I don't mind doing this right here on the street, but to avoid getting into trouble maybe we should take this inside your truck at least."

Zandria bit her lip and nodded her head in agreement. She pulled her keys out of her little black clutch, hit the unlock button twice and opened the passenger side door. She gestured for Annaca to climb up into the truck. Annaca grinned as she climbed into the front bench seat, sliding in backwards so she could face Zandria.

Zandria beamed up at her as she climbed up into the truck. A bit clumsy but eager, she pushed Annaca back and climbed on top of Annaca, mounting her like a wild mare. She leaned forward and started kissing Annaca vigorously. She was new to this concept, but she was blissfully diving in feet first.

Annaca admired her hunger, but she had to slow her down so they could both enjoy this. Annaca wanted to taste her. She wanted to caress her body with her tongue. Annaca seduced her with words and sensual notions from the beginning. Now, she had to follow through on her enticing verbal promises. She wanted to enjoy this first-time occurrence and set a high standard for Zandria. The *first time* always leaves a lasting impression, good, bad or otherwise.

Annaca cupped Zandria's face in her hands and said, " Honey, I love your enthusiasm, but let's slow this down a notch. I want you to enjoy it, and I want to make a good impression on you."

Zandria smirked and replied, "Okay, I understand. Thank you."

Annaca ran her hands down from Zandria's face to her sides. Slowly, Annaca lifted Zandria's top. Zandria smiled and stretched her arms upwards so Annaca could remove it. Desire flashed in Zandria's eyes as she brought her arms down and placed her hands on Annaca's soft breasts. She started rubbing them and pulling at Annaca's dress top with inexperienced hands.

Annaca stared up at her with amusement. Zandria was so innocent and sweet with a kinky side waiting to get out. Annaca pulled her down to kiss her sweet lips, and Zandria's hips ground against Annaca. The heat of their bodies fogged up the glass in the truck. Zandria moved from Annaca's lips to her cheek and then traveled down to her neck. Zandria's hands wandered all over, trying to map out Annaca's figure.

Annaca decided it was time to take control and give Zandria some ideas for later. She slowed Zandria down as she graciously turned her over onto her back. Annaca mounted Zandria with ease. The seat belt buckle was partially digging into her left knee cap but she was too occupied to pay attention to it.

She scooted Zandria up until her head was resting on the driver's side armrest. This gave her plenty of room to tease and please Zandria. Annaca's hands immediately went for Zandria's mini skirt so she could ease it up. As it slid up past her hips, Zandria's white and black satin panties were revealed and in her way.

Zandria ran her finger across her bottom lip and then bit her lip while she watched Annaca inch her panties down.

Zandria propped her right leg up and let her left leg dropped onto the floorboard to give Annaca a bit more room to move. She awaited Annaca's touch and the heat of her breath.

Annaca grinned as she watched Zandria's anticipation grow. She knew what she wanted, and it was only a matter of seconds before she would have her moaning in the sweetest ecstasy. With her index finger, Annaca slowly traced a circle around Zandria's hips and down the crease of her legs to watch her flinch.

Zandria's legs spread further apart, begging for more. Her right leg was now braced against the seat. Annaca's devious grin grew into a smile as she sucked on her finger. She ran the tip of her wet finger across Zandria's clit. Zandria let out a gasp. She scooted closer to Annaca, begging for more with her body.

Annaca was pleased with her reaction. Annaca pulled her fingers to her mouth to taste her and re-lubricate her fingers to ease her teasing touch. She licked her thumb and gently started to massage her clit. Zandria gripped the seat and threw her head back in tortured ecstasy. Annaca slowly inserted her fingers into Zandria while continuing to move her thumb in circular motions.

Zandria let out a high-pitched whimper, "Oh God!"

Annaca leaned in with her right hand and pinched Zandria's perky nipple. She rolled one between her fingers. Zandria's hips gyrated into Annaca's hand as Annaca paced her thrusts. Zandria bit her lip seductively as she watched Annaca tease her body. Annaca looked down at her fingers playing with Zandria and got a pang of excitement. She leaned down and pulled her fingers back so she could taste this sweet little cherry.

Zandria wanted to tease Annaca in return, but she couldn't get her hands to unclench from the seat. She looked down to see Annaca's head lift as she slid her fingers back into her. Zandria was soaked and about to get off any second. Just the sight of another girl licking her clit was making her explode.

With every penetration of Annaca's fingers, Zandria moaned with pleasure. Annaca slowly withdrew her fingers and bowed down to entice her again. Annaca extended her tongue out as she licked Zandria's sweet center. The tip of her tongue flicked her clit, and Zandria let out a shrieking groan. Suddenly, Zandria's hands released the seat and entangled in Annaca's long ebony hair.

She continued to tease and taunt her with her tongue, listening for squeals of pleasure and feeling the grip tighten on the back of her head. Zandria's thighs tensed around Annaca's head. She was getting close to climax. Zandria let out a glass-shattering squeal as she squeezed her thighs tight enough to block the sound from Annaca.

Annaca continued taunting with mini flicks of her tongue just to feel Zandria's body shudder below her. Zandria's sweet juices were dripping from Annaca's chin as she looked up to smile at her. Annaca wiped her face with her forearm.

Zandria laid there for a moment as Annaca was grinning up at her. She continued to twitch a bit.

"That was probably the quickest orgasm I have ever received. How did you learn how to do that?" Zandria questioned.

Annaca's grin widened into a smile as she replied, "Well, I just do what I want to have done to me, and it seems to work out pretty well, I would say."

Zandria reached for Annaca and pulled her up to sit on her chest. Annaca re-positioned herself. She braced against the driver's door with her knees buried into the seat, straddling Zandria's head.

Annaca looked down. "What are your intentions, young lady?"

Zandria grinned up at her as she slipped her hands up Annaca's dress, searching for a pair of panties to remove.

"I think I'm about to return the favor." She replied.

Annaca braced herself as the lustful desire raced through her. She got a twinge of excitement surging between her legs. Zandria used her fingers to remove the black lace g-string that was in her way. Annaca obliged by maneuvering around to help. Zandria had only felt her own gem, so she explored Annaca's soft skin and wet center with her fingers. Zandria's icy touch made Annaca flinch.

Annaca gripped the door to keep her balance. Zandria grabbed Annaca's ass and pulled her straight to her mouth. She swirled her tongue around and gently sucked on her clit. Annaca tightened her muscles to increase the feel of Zandria's taunting tongue. Zandria's nails dug into Annaca's ass as she pulled her closer. She wanted to lick every bit of her and make Annaca squirm. She suckled on her clit with pulsing flicks.

Zandria released an ass cheek and pulled her hand forward. Her finger traced Annaca's inner sweet spot. Gently, she slipped her finger into Annaca as she wiggled it around until she found the spot so often missed. Annaca let out a groaning sigh. Zandria kept pressing the spot and tortured Annaca's clit with her tongue.

Annaca was so close to squeezing Zandria's fingers off with her muscles. Her body locked up into a shuddering orgasm that, when she released, her head hit the driver's side window. The pain in her head had nothing on the pleasure in her loins.

The girls were tuned into each other so much that they didn't notice their audience that watched with envy. Jamie had closed the bar and walked out to find the girls entangled in the front seat of Zandria's truck. They had left the door open so anyone who passed by got a show. Jamie and a regular who hung out occasionally stood back against the wall and watched the show.

They had a full view, with the streetlight above posing as a spotlight. They kept quiet just enough not to get caught, but both became uncomfortably horny by the live-action porn they witnessed.

After Annaca had climaxed, Jamie gave it a few seconds before he made his presence known. He walked up to the truck door and cleared his throat. Both girls jumped at the sound.

Jamie laughed and said, "Well, Ms. Annaca, it would appear your fear of public places is nonexistent. You left the door open, and we got quite a show. Bravo, girls, now I need a cold shower unless you want to come back to my place for seconds."

Annaca laughed and blushed but wasn't really embarrassed at being caught. It turned her on even more. Zandria didn't seem to mind either. Both girls adjusted themselves and plopped down on the seat of the truck. The guys stood at the door of the truck while they teased and joked with the girls for a few minutes. The thought of another round did intrigue Annaca, but Zandria seemed to want to call it a night.

Annaca hopped out of the truck and stood next to Jamie. She motioned for Zandria to come to her. Zandria climbed out of the truck to the edge of the seat where she sat down and waited with her feet dangling at the rim of the door frame. Annaca couldn't resist, so she stepped up to Zandria and pulled her into a kiss.

Zandria returned the kiss by cupping Annaca's face in her hands and pulling her closer. The guys made catcalls and whistling noises. The girls broke the kiss and giggled.

Annaca said her goodbyes to Zandria.

"If you are interested, you have my number now; call any-time. There are always other places to repeat this evening without an audience." As she gestured to the men standing next to the truck.

Zandria grinned at her and nodded. Annaca stepped back and shut the passenger door. Zandria started up her truck with a low grumble and drove off into the early morning.

Jamie grinned at Annaca with a knowing smirk. Annaca looked at him and shrugged her shoulders, "What, are you jealous?"

Jamie shook his head and said, "Not at all, I got to watch the whole thing."

Annaca shook her head and replied, "Well, I can't help that I draw both sexes in. Do you want a kiss for a taste?"

Jamie grabbed Annaca and pulled her in for a kiss.

The regular, Michael, shook his head and said, "I will just head home now."

Still locked in the kiss, they both waved as he walked away.

Jamie decided he would be slick, so he hoisted Annaca up and she wrapped her legs around his waist. Jamie slowly walked toward the building while kissing her and holding her up. Thud, Annaca's back hit the building as he braced her against the wall. Annaca had a twisted thought run through her head as she kissed Jamie.

I have done this before; I just hope that I don't get left hanging again. She thought.

Jamie tried bracing her body with his hips so he could use his hands for other activities. He had nothing in his way since Annaca's g-string still resided in Zandria's truck. Jamie slipped his finger into Annaca, and she gasped.

"That feels nice, but I really need something more." Annaca whispered in his ear.

"You know how to get what you want, and I'm already hard just from watching you." Jamie whispered back.

Annaca gripped him with her legs and squeezed her hand between them to unbutton his jeans. She held the material in her hands as she yanked. The button released, and the zipper came down in one swift motion. Jamie grinned at her and reached down to adjust his throbbing member.

He slowly adjusted his hips so he could slip inside her. He started with mini thrusts to inch his way in. With the first full thrust, Annaca felt her back scrape against the wall, but she didn't care. She let out a deep sigh and bit down on his neck. Jamie jammed his pelvis into her as she bit down. Annaca dug into his back with her nails and bit harder. Jamie plunged deeper, giving it all he had to give.

Heavily, he groaned as he gave her exactly what she wanted to finish out her night. His body quivered under her, and his arms shot to the wall for stability. Annaca hung onto him with her legs wrapped around his waist and her arms around his neck with her nails embedded into his back. His breaths were short and quick as sweat was dripping down his face. Annaca loosened her grip on his neck and gently kissed the mark that was bleeding.

Shaking, Jamie pulled Annaca away from the wall and put her down on her feet. She brushed her dress down as he worked on zipping his pants up. She leaned back against the wall and grinned at Jamie. He looked worn out and ready for bed now.

"I wasn't expecting that, but it was well worth being the second act." Jamie snickered.

Annaca shook her head and replied, "I guess I should go home and get a shower. I'm good for the moment, so I can hopefully go to bed."

Jamie leaned over and kissed her cheek, gave a little wave and headed back to his vehicle. Annaca began her walk to her flat as she reflected on the events that took place. She was feeling brave, so she stopped and removed her shoes to feel the cold pavement under her feet.

She listened to the sounds of the early morning as she walked home. Vehicles were driving by, and someone honked at her as she reached her door. She didn't bother to look because it didn't sound like they were stopping. Unlocking the bottom door that opened up to her stairs, she stepped inside.

Climbing the stairs, she reached her top door and unlocked it as well. She opened it and put her shoes down by the door, leaving a trail of her clothing as she walked to her bed. She smiled as she looked down at Jack.

Kissing her fingers, and placed them to his tank and said, "Good night little man, I love you."

Standing there completely nude, she flopped down onto her bed, rolled up in her comforter and passed out.

Chapter Fifteen

Sweet Return

Weston had been gone for some time now. Annaca wondered if she would ever see him again. Regardless of whom she occupied her time with, she still wanted Weston. He was the one who started this desire and kicked it into overdrive. He was always on her mind and in her dreams. Austin was a close second to Weston.

It was hard to decide, but she wasn't ready to just drop everything and settle down. She was young and had a career to focus on. Eventually, she wanted to buy a house in the country and maybe raise a family. The *Dream* Life, as most would refer to it.

It was February, and Valentine's Day was right around the corner. Makko's was hosting a Valentine's Day party called a stoplight party. They had red cups for taken, yellow cups for proceed with caution and green for good to go. It was a cute gimmick idea for a party. It didn't alienate single people.

The party date had finally rolled around, and Annaca hoped she would run into someone she knew there. She was on her own at the party. Carlene hooked up with that stripper, Trevor, and they seemed to be hitting it off well. She hadn't heard from anyone really, so she was on the hunt for someone new. She needed an orgasmic fix, and though she hated this holiday, she figured someone had to be in the same boat as her.

Annaca decided to wear her garnet cocktail halter dress with matching open toed ankle strap stilettos. Her ebony hair draped down her back. A sterling silver chain hung around her neck with an intricate Celtic heart for cleavage decoration. Her dress hugged her figure perfectly. She was looking for attention one way or another.

She was on fire for the party, and she couldn't wait to see who her next target would be. As she walked around Makko's, both guys and girls were checking her up and down. She was enjoying the fact that she was catching people staring at her.

The party cups were placed in a cute display on the bar for customers to choose their color. Jamie was training a new guy and showing him the regulars as they came in. Alex was young and new to the bartender scene. He seemed to catch on quickly. Jamie didn't seem to get frustrated with him at all, despite it being his first night.

Annaca glanced around before she took a seat at the bar. Jamie smiled at her and introduced her to Alex. Annaca flashed a smile and shook his hand. He had floppy, sandy blond hair, blue eyes and chubby cheeks that anyone would want to pinch. Alex was average looking, but he was quick witted. He was cracking jokes to cover up the fact that he was nervous.

Annaca enjoyed the banter between the three of them while she drank from a green cup. Occasionally, she looked around the room, checking to see if there were any other green cups of interest. She was hoping for another night of enchanting fantasy, but it was starting to look like another sexless night. Sometimes a girl just strikes out, and she was okay with it, but the touch of another, she often desired.

The night had rounded a little after midnight. Annaca was ready to call it a night and just go home to climb into some comfy sleep clothes. It was still chilly out, so she had no problem snuggling up with a good book in her comfy bed, reading to Jack and drifting off into another inevitable wet dream.

Annaca sighed to herself as she told Jamie and Alex that she was headed home. She had some fun for the night, but she was going to turn in early. The guys gave her pouty faces, but they understood. She paid her tab when she ordered one more shot to keep her warm for the walk home. She got up, waved to the guys and headed toward the glass doors.

As she opened the right-side glass door, there stood a tall and handsome man with a bouquet of a dozen red roses. The bouquet was encased elegantly in shimmering lace and accented with sprigs of baby's breath. Annaca gasped when she realized who was standing in front of her. She couldn't believe her eyes, it had been a while since she had seen him. Of all days, she never expected to see him standing in front of her with a dozen roses for someone else.

It was Austin. He had a date with a blond who had been sitting at a table by herself waiting for him to get out of work. She was country cute with brown square boots, a light blue jean mini skirt and an open flannel cover shirt that hid a red tank top.

He sheepishly grinned at her and asked how she was doing.

Annaca shrugged her shoulders and said, "I'm good. I'm going home. There's nothing here for me."

Austin tried to explain the situation, but she really didn't want to hear it. She was ready to go home and sulk in her bed with a good book.

"Look, it's no big deal. It's not like we were dating or anything. My man Jack is waiting for me to get home, anyway." She said as she excused herself from the awkward conversation.

She could hear him calling her name in the distance, but what was the point? It would just be weird, and she didn't need that right now.

She picked up her pace on her way back to her flat. The clicking sound of her heels hitting the sidewalk was comforting because it meant that she was closer to her little piece of heaven. Thoughts kept running through her head about her country night with Austin, but she tried to shake them. It was just an adventure and nothing more. She didn't want to be haunted by her thoughts; she just wanted to be snuggled down in her bed.

This hallmark holiday was a joke to her, anyway. Why would people show their affection for only one day of the year when it should be every day? It should be because they want to. She hated how holidays felt like a deadline instead of a celebration. Not to mention the fact that Valentine's Day was originally about a feast in honor of a martyr and then publicized by a massacre, then turned into a commercialized reason to buy chocolates, flowers and jewelry.

Annaca looked up to see the theater. It was dark, but she could swear there was someone sitting in front of her door. The closer she got, the more visible the figure that darkened her doorstep became. A mysterious man was propped up against her flat entrance holding an enormous bouquet. His boots rested on the sidewalk, and it appeared that he was asleep. Annaca got about ten feet away, and it was clear who was waiting for her.

Weston was sitting on the steps holding a bouquet of crimson roses and ivory lilies tied together with a bright red satin ribbon. Behind the bouquet, there sat a cute little pearly white teddy bear with a pink heart nose and red paw prints.

Annaca shook her head as she walked up to him. She stood there for a moment to see if he was sleeping.

Weston tipped up his cowboy hat and asked, "Will you be my Valentine, Ms. Annaca?"

Annaca stepped back and crossed her arms as she looked down at him and stated, "I don't know, you have been gone again without a word. What makes you think you can show up with flowers and a cute bear to win me over? Besides, I hate Valentine's Day. You should give gifts because you want to, not because the calendar says so."

Weston grinned up at her and stood up.

He offered the gifts to her and said, "well darlin', I am truly sorry for the lack of my communication. When I'm in the country, my family and the farm are my priorities. I am just trying to make up for my absence and hope that you can understand and forgive me. We don't have a true arrangement or relationship, but I am offering my time only to you when I'm in the city."

Annaca wasn't sure how to respond. This must be too good to be true. She wasn't ready to attach herself to just one person, but she definitely enjoyed having his attention when he was in town. Annaca instantly caved in like a lovesick girl. Trying to juggle the flowers and bear, she motioned for him to follow her upstairs.

He offered to carry the flowers since they were so bulky and awkward. As they ascended the stairs, Weston complimented her dress and asked if there was a chance of removing it for her.

Annaca snickered and responded with, "That's a little forward of you."

Weston winced and said, "I'm sorry. I didn't mean to overstep. Do you forgive me?"

Annaca laughed and said, "You goofball. I'm not mad or offended. Relax. I was kind of hoping you would help me remove my dress because the zipper on this thing is a pain in the ass."

Weston grinned and said, "As you wish, m'lady. I'm all yours to do whatever you want to do to me."

A sinister smile grew across Annaca's face as ideas formed in her head. She wanted him to ravish her body, yet she also wanted to have a sweet and sensual evening with the man that frequented her dreams.

They entered her flat. She retrieved the flowers from Weston and placed them on the counter in her kitchen. She searched her cabinets for a vase, trimmed the stems, and filled the vase with cold water, placing them it in her kitchen window.

She turned around and faced Weston. Weston glanced around the room and noticed Jack.

"So, uh, when did you get a pet fish?" He asked.

Annaca smiled and said, "Well, I was waiting to see you at the festival that you never showed up at. I ran into a guy who had also been stood up by his date. We rode rides together, and he won me a fish at one of the ring toss games. That fish is my main man. His name is Jack."

Weston shrugged and said, "Well, I don't think he will be much competition, but I will put up a fight for your attention tonight. I think I still have a fishing pole in my truck."

Annaca raised an eyebrow at him and stated, "You are not fighting or catching my fish. He is here to stay despite anyone who comes in and out of my life."

Weston grabbed his chest playfully and responded, "Ouch, straight through the heart, huntress."

Annaca palmed her forehead, rolled her eyes while she walked towards him. Weston stood there looking damn good in his hat. It had been so long since she had seen him. She ignored his goofy attempt to be funny as she jumped on him and wrapped her legs around him as they tumbled to the ground.

He landed on his back to protect her from the fall. She squeezed him tighter with her legs as she grabbed his face and crushed her mouth to his willing one. Although he was notorious for always going missing, she wanted this man tonight. She ground her hips into his as she felt a slight rise of approval.

Annaca started tearing at his clothes and trying to strip them off him. She wanted to feel the heat of his body. He was playfully resisting her desire by trying to get away and acting as though he didn't really want anything. She pulled her knees in to grip him with her thighs, squeezing his ribs. He let out a little groan.

He laughed at her and rolled her over, caging her in his arms to protect her. She wrapped her arms around his neck to pull him back into another kiss.

Weston broke out of the kiss to say. "You know, I can't give you anything permanent right now, but eventually, I will."

Annaca leaned back on the floor with a bit of an attitude. "Well, unless you are proposing, shut up and kiss me. I am not concerned about future promises. Right now, I just want you inside me."

Weston shook his head and replied, "Girl, I am trying to tell you that I only want you. I want to be with you. I just can't right now."

Annaca pouted and snapped back with, "Well, I just want to fuck and I don't want empty promises because you can't always be here when I need you. I'm not expecting anything more than sex. We don't make love, we have sex, and then you take off."

Weston's face went from serious to almost tearful as Annaca reached for his face and said, "Look, I understand what you are trying to say and I appreciate it, but truth is, you have responsibilities and so do I. Can't we just have tonight and we can worry about the other stuff later?"

Weston seemed to agree with her statement as he leaned in and kissed her like the first time. Annaca wanted more of that. She hungrily kissed him back, wrapping her arms around his neck to pull him in tight. Weston pulled back, but coaxed her to follow him.

"How about we take this to the bed? I don't want to wear holes in your floor or my knees." Weston joked.

Annaca chuckled and agreed. Weston swiped her up in his arms and placed her on the bed. He pulled his shirt off, playfully stripped his belt off and dropped his pants. He had on one of those red g-strings that said, *Be Mine*.

Annaca laughed loudly and responded with, "Always. Now get over here and help me get this damn dress off."

Weston bowed and replied, "As you wish, m'lady."

Annaca sat up and turned around so Weston could unzip her dress. He spread the dress apart to show her tender back. He trailed his fingers down to watch her shiver from his touch. Weston pushed her down so he could remove the rest of the dress. He pulled it down her legs and past her feet.

All she had left was a matching garnet thong. His big warm hands caressed her cheeks. He pulled one hand back to give her a little swat. Then he slid his finger into the band of her thong and whipped it off. Annaca looked back at him, waiting to see what he would do next.

He placed his hands on her hips, encouraging her to slide to the edge of the bed. He kept rubbing her ass waiting for her to get into position. She was arched up in doggie style, but that wasn't what he was giving her. She felt his fingers reach her stomach and slowly drag back. He felt his way around until he stopped to insert a finger into her.

Annaca let out a quiet gasp of approval. He gently slid in a second finger as Annaca tightened up. She was already wet just from him playing with her. She felt his fingers leave her. He grabbed her hips, pulling her up a bit, and then he slid himself into her.

Annaca moaned as he continued to slip in and out of her. With his next thrust, he smacked her ass cheek hard enough to leave a bruise. Annaca about came right there. He pulled out and slammed into her again. She could tell he was close to getting off because he pulled out again. Before she knew it, she was being flipped over onto her back.

She looked up at him as she asked, "Are we in an aggressive mood tonight?"

He smiled at her with a toothy grin and replied, "Maybe. Would that be a bad thing?"

Annaca shook her head. Then she asked, "Do I need to give you a safe word?"

His smile widened, and he replied, "Do you even have a safe word?"

Annaca grinned up at him and said, "Well, no. I have never needed one before."

With that said, he took a step back and replied, "Maybe I shouldn't tonight. You don't seem interested." He said playfully.

She gave him a dirty look as she sat up and reached for him. He pulled out of her grasp, trying to play hard to get. Smirking down at her, grabbed her ankles and pulled her feet up to his shoulders. He lifted her ass up into position and stuck a finger in to check to see if she was still wet.

She gasped at his touch. He grinned at the sound she made as he pulled his finger out and glided into her again. Annaca gripped the bed trying to hold on. He continued to slide in and out so slowly, she grew impatient. She enjoyed the teasing in this game that they were playing, but she desired the release. She wanted him slamming into her.

Weston could feel her impatience, and he enjoyed watching her get frustrated from his teasing. He pulled out of her, set her feet down, and he got down on his knees. He decided he would give her a little taste of what he wanted to do to her body. Gently he started to kiss the inside of her thighs.

She shivered under him with every touch. His lips were warm against her cool skin. His mouth watered at the thought of tasting her. A drip of saliva landed on her clit as he opened his mouth to entice her with his tongue. Softly, he fluttered his tongue up and down against her clit. She released her grip on the bed and clasped her hands at the back of his head.

Weston gently stuck his tongue in and out of her, occasionally licking his way around and stopping at her clit. He had barely begun, but her legs began trembling beneath him. He enjoyed the sharp pangs he felt in his head as she dug her nails into his scalp. It only made him tease her more.

Bracing himself with his right arm, he brought his left hand up to extend his pleasing torment. She drew in a deep breath through her nose as he slid his first two fingers into her. He pushed upward, looking for that notorious spot that makes her squeal. As he hit it, she moaned and rocked her hips with the motion of his fingers. Her muscles locked down, which made it difficult for him to move his fingers. He pulled his fingers out of her womanly grasp and smiled at her.

She opened her eyes and looked at him. "Is there a problem?" She asked.

"No, ma'am, I just had to get the feeling back into my fingers." He joked.

Annaca had enough of this teasing, she wanted control. She sat up and pulled at him to get up onto the bed. He laughed at her as she tried.

"What are you trying to do?" He asked.

She huffed at him and said, "I want to be on top and ride you. I'm attempting to take control of this situation, and I'm failing miserably."

Weston laughed at her and gave in so she wouldn't get mad at him. He clambered onto the bed and flopped onto his back as she mounted him like a stallion. He grabbed his cock and held it in place to make sure it went where it was supposed to go. Annaca stopped mid-drop and pulled back. She sat down on his thighs and bent forward.

She licked her lips and began to tease the tip with her tongue. He already had it in place; she figured it would be best to prime him completely before she took what she wanted. His eyes rolled into the back of his head as the heat of her mouth enticed the blood to rush to the tip.

"Oh Fuck!" He groaned out.

He moaned with each twist of her tongue as it traveled up and down his shaft. He placed his hands on the back of her head and began to run his fingers through her hair. She used her fingers to press into his pressure points just at the meeting of his sack and shaft with her thumb and wrapped her other two fingers behind his balls, applying pressure.

He sucked in a loud gasp of air, and his whole body locked up. She brought him to the brink of climax and stopped.

"That will teach you to tease me." She added.

But she couldn't stop there. She licked the tip and re-positioned herself to actually mount and ride the hell out of him. As she lowered herself down onto him, he grabbed her hips and guided her onto him. She gripped him with her knees and tucked her feet under his thighs in case he got the idea to buck her off.

As she rocked back and forth, she could feel all the blood pumping straight to his cock. Annaca welcomed the increase in his already pulsating length. Annaca tightened her muscles trying to squeeze as hard as she could. Weston let out a moan and said, "Oh god you feel so good!"

He started thrusting faster as Annaca reached for his hand. She wanted him to rub her clit. She wanted to get off so badly. Annaca's eyes closed as she tipped her head back, grinding into him as hard as she could. They couldn't hold out anymore. They both started quivering with ecstasy. Annaca felt that familiar warming sensation as she climaxed.

Weston shuddered under her while sporadically thrusting. Annaca waited for him to stop jolting. Annaca leaned forward to lie on his chest. She started tracing little hearts onto his chest as she sat up and asked, "So, round two?"

Weston laughed and smacked his forehead. "You are going to have to give me a minute. I think you just pulled every drop out of me." He responded.

Annaca shrugged her shoulders and said jokingly, "Happy Valentine's Day?"

"What about a shower, maybe something to eat and then round two?" Annaca proposed as she got off the bed.

Weston laughed and sighed, "There is just no pleasing you for more than five minutes."

Annaca grinned and replied, "I like multiple pleasures. What's wrong with that?"

Weston shook his head, rolled his eyes at her and replied, "There is nothing wrong with wanting to be pleased. You keep me on my toes every time. I will never be bored with you."

Annaca smiled. "Good, so how about that shower?"

Weston rubbed his face and then stretched out across her bed. "I suppose a shower would be a good start."

Weston stood up and walked over to Annaca and wrapped her in his arms. Annaca leaned in to kiss his neck then, decided to bite down instead, sucking the blood to the surface of his skin. She felt like doing some damage since he was such a tease earlier.

Weston didn't stop her. He tightened his grip as Annaca dug her nails into his sides. His cock stood at attention and was ready for another round. Annaca released her grip as she felt him rising to the occasion.

Weston pulled away, looked down and said, "Well, it looks like you found my trigger."

Annaca, pleased with her damage. She smiled up at him and said, "I'm ready for that shower now."

Chapter Sixteen

Lust Not Love

As the water rained down on their bodies, Annaca sweetly smiled up at him as he bent down to kiss her. He lifted her up and locked her in his arms as he passionately nibbled down from her cheek to her sensitive neck. She nuzzled her face into the nape of his neck, breathing in the scent of her soap on his skin, as she gently laved the damage she had caused to his skin. He playfully growled at the touch of her lips.

His grip was slightly slipping due to the water as he set her back down and cupped her face, pulling her into another deep kiss. She wrapped her arms around his waist as he deepened the already passion filled kiss. The steam wafted around their slick bodies and masked the heat of his breath. With each touch of his lips to her skin, shivers went down her spine and goose bumps rose all over her body. This man knew he had her wrapped around his little finger with each deep sensual kiss that made her toes curl.

She didn't know it yet, but she couldn't keep all her emotions hidden when it came to him. He softly kissed her lips one last time and ended it with a suggestion that they finish up their shower before the hot water ran out. Annaca agreed, and they soaped each other up only to rinse off and get out.

Annaca got out first so she could grab a couple of towels. She wrapped her towel around her wet body and waited for him. He stood there all proud, waiting for her to stop staring and hand over the towel. He was already standing at attention again. She just stood there and admired his gorgeous body.

He thought he would try to get a smile out of her, so he told her he could hold his towel with no hands. She raised an eyebrow and said, "Oh?"

He shook out his towel and hung it on his proud cock. Using his core muscles, he waved the towel up and down.

Annaca laughed and shook her head. "You are such a goof-ball."

He smirked at her and then dried off. He quickly leaned in and kissed her cheek as he wrapped the fuzzy towel around his waist.

She reached for his towel and tugged gently as she led the way to her bed. "So, are you actually going to stay with me tonight?" she asked.

He looked crestfallen as he hung his head and said that he couldn't. She picked up a pillow and threw it at him.

"When will I get to wake up in your arms at least once?" She questioned.

He caught the pillow and shrugged his shoulders. "I'm not certain. The farm is never-ending. I don't have any control over that, so I sneak in what time I can, just to see you. Maybe you'd want to take a break from here and come with me?" He asked.

She gaped at him for a second and asked, "Are you suggesting I come to your place and meet your parents?"

He shrugged again and replied, "Yeah, I guess I am."

Annaca was shocked. *He just asked me to meet his parents.* She thought.

She was excited at the thought, but fear swept over her at the same time. *This was a whole additional step in their game of chase. Was he serious or just saying it to appease her about his never staying with her?* Her mind was racing with questions now. She entertained the idea of going out to the farm and seeing his side of the world. She really could use a small vacation to get away, and maybe she would have him all to herself.

She knew he worked a lot on the farm, but he couldn't work all day and night. Either way, she looked forward to the getaway.

She perked up and said, "I will have to check my calendar and make sure I can take the time off. We don't have any major projects in the works right now. The only stipulation is that I would have to put in to ask for the time off. So it would be at least two weeks before I could take a week off. How does that sound?" She inquired.

He smiled at her and walked over to sit next to her on her bed. "It sounds like a wonderful plan. I'm not positive how well it will go, but we can try it out. I just don't want you to get bored out there when I'm working. There isn't much for you to do out there."

She kissed him and pushed him down onto her bed. Boredom wasn't a concern. She would figure it out. She climbed on top of him.

He gripped her ass and said, "I really love this ass of yours."

She smirked at him and kissed him again. "I really love kissing you. Actually, let's pull that four-letter word out before it causes trouble. I don't want you to get all emotional on me and falling for me." She said saucily.

He laughed at her for being afraid of a word. He knew that she felt it already and was trying desperately to hide any emotion other than lust.

She gave him a dirty look and said, "Last time I said it, I had an unpleasant experience. A relationship nightmare, if you will. I enjoy what we have, and I just don't want it to ruin what we have going on."

He shrugged and said, "It's okay. I won't say it like that anymore. But I am obsessed with your body, and that isn't going to change. I hope you can at least deal with that."

She poked him in the chest and asked if he was sure he had to go that night.

He grinned at her and said, "I'll tell you what, I will stay until seven, but then I have to get back; no later."

She accepted that for now even though she wanted so much more than she was willing to admit.

Annaca smiled and then urged him to get up on the bed with her. She wanted to be held for a little fleeting moment. She knew it wasn't going to last, but what could it hurt? He curled up with her at the head of the bed. He was bigger than her, so she didn't need a pillow. She snuggled into the crook of his arm and laid her left arm across his chest.

She grazed her hand back and forth across his chest as he played with her damp hair. The feeling of him running his hands through her hair relaxed her. She couldn't fight the exhaustion that caught up with her. Within five minutes of him playing with her hair, she was fast asleep in his muscular embrace.

Weston remained with her and continued to play with her hair while she slept. He was amazed by how cute she was when she slept. He didn't want to hurt Annaca; he was falling for her, but she was stern about that four-letter word.

Maybe a visit to the farm might pull the city out of her. She might enjoy it out there, he thought.

He knew she was wild still, but sometimes he almost felt as though she felt the same way about him. He wanted to give her as much time as she needed. This girl rocked his world, and he didn't want it to change.

Weston's alarm went off at 6:30 am. Blaring "Reveille," the military wake-up bugle solo. Annaca didn't even flinch. Weston jumped up and rushed to shut it off so it wouldn't wake her up. Annaca rolled over onto her right side and continued to snooze away.

A wave of relief washed over him. He couldn't be late, and he really didn't want to argue with her about more time. He rushed around gathering up his clothes and putting them on, as he looked over at her and she was still asleep.

Man, she sleeps hard. He thought.

He walked over to her bed, leaned in and kissed her forehead gently.

He whispered, "I will see you soon, my love."

He leaned up and turned to walk out as he grabbed his boots that were at the door. Easing the door open, he looked back at her one last time and he was gone again.

Annaca's alarm sounded with a standard ringtone from her phone. She stretched out and reached for Weston. He had left, and he didn't even say goodbye. She pouted for a moment and continued to stretch and wake up. She had started out in a towel but it was tangled among her comforter now.

She pulled the sheet off her bed and went into the kitchen to get herself a cup of coffee and check her phone for anything important. She had hoped Weston had at least sent her a text to say when he would be back in town, but he didn't. It was his usual act of him bolting for a long time and no response. She was getting used to it, even though it was a twinge of pain when she truly thought about it.

Thoughts of the conversation they had the night before floated through her mind. *I sure hope he was serious about this trip to the farm. I can keep myself busy with work on my laptop, so I don't know why he would be worried about me being bored. Hell, I'll even chip in and help. I don't mind. I need this break, and I will be with him. Maybe we will actually get closer. I might get to know him more than just his body.*

Annaca shook her head to clear her thoughts and went to her closet to get dressed. She tossed her sheet onto her bed and gathered her stuff for her day. She didn't really have to do much, turn in a couple of reports and run some errands. It would maybe take a couple of hours.

She checked around her flat to make sure everything was in order, and she caught a glimpse of the towel that Weston had used. It was in the laundry basket in the bathroom. A flash of their performance went through her mind, and she got a twinge of excitement between her legs. She was ready for another round of his teasing and pleasing.

The thought of his strength to just roll her around and his gentle touch as he kissed her body, sent her mind into a whirlwind. She couldn't wait to feel his embrace and gentle kisses all over her body. She desired to kiss his lips and feel his body against hers. Not to mention the ability that his tongue possessed. The idea sent a tingling sensation through her whole body. She was definitely in lust with that man's body and pleasing ways.

She shook her head to clear her mind, and she grabbed her keys off the rack. She walked out and locked her door behind her. It was time to get back to reality and do the grown-up thing that all adults groan about. She walked down her stairs to her bottom door, walked through the door and spun around to lock it as well. Spinning back around, she looked out into the city. With a heavy sigh, she headed toward the bus.

Chapter Seventeen

Hello Doctor Main

It was supposed to be spring, but it was freezing outside. It was the end of March, and the sun was setting on a Sunday evening as Annaca stayed home to enjoy some alone time. She was sitting on the steps outside her flat, wrapped up in her favorite fleece blanket, holding a cup of creamy hot cocoa.

Occasionally, she got lost in the swirl of her cup as she sat, people watching and hoping to stargaze. It was difficult to see the stars in town with the dim orange glow of the streetlights. She would love to have another night out in an open field, where she could stargaze like she did as a child. Some of her best childhood memories were in the countryside at her parents' plantation style house.

A faint childhood memory flashed into her mind as she could almost feel the warmth of a summer night with a vision of lightning bugs speckling the dark ground. She was daydreaming of being in the countryside on a clear night, stars decorating the night sky with a guest appearance of the moon showing different phases each night.

She was a person who enjoyed the peacefulness of the dark; not much of an opportunity for it in the city. Her mind wandered to Weston and what he was doing at the farm tonight. She longed to see him. He was the last person to touch her the way she desired, and she couldn't help but crave his body entangled with hers.

She never put in her notice at work because she had no clue when he would show back up in her life. She wanted his touch desperately, but she couldn't count on his communication. By now, her flowers had wilted and died. Her bear sat on her bookshelf and kept watch over her while it collected dust. There wasn't a call or text from him, and she wasn't holding her breath. It was just her and Jack, her main fish.

The last few weeks, she hadn't been feeling herself. She spent a great deal of time just watching Jack swim around his little tank while she rested in bed. She was exhausted, or she was starving, or she couldn't keep anything down at all. Maybe she was coming down with her usual spring flu that liked to kick her butt for a month straight.

She figured it was time to make a doctor's appointment and see what Dr. Main thought was going on. She made a mental note to call and set up an appointment in the morning.

She gazed up at the sky a little longer before she turned in for the night. Worn down, she sauntered up her stairs and dumped out her cold cocoa in the kitchen sink. She turned on the faucet and swirled water around her cup to keep it from being sticky. Peering into her bedroom, her bed looked inviting.

She dragged her feet as she walked over to her bed and sat down. She kissed her fingers and touched the glass of Jack's tank and then climbed in and snuggled up with her blankets. Thoughts of her ideal man drifted through her mind as she warmed up with her favorite comforter.

She was sitting on the windowsill of her flat, reading a book, when he barged in through her door. She jumped and dropped her book when she realized who it was. Weston had busted in. He rushed over to her, swept her up into his arms and carried her over to the bed. She wrapped her arms around his neck and immediately started kissing him. She was ecstatic to see him. He laid her down on the bed, gently kissing her lips and then pulling away. He stood up and ripped his shirt off, following up with removing his pants.

She was shocked at how fast he was going, but she didn't care, he was here, and that's all that mattered. She wanted any time she could get from him. He climbed on top of her and started kissing her neck and pulling at her clothes. He wanted her stripped, and he wasn't slowing down or taking no for an answer.

She was intrigued by his aggression. She wanted more of it. He helped her remove her clothing and continued kissing her neck. He leaned up and nibbled on her ear and then commenced sucking on her neck. The sensation was enthralling, but she had to stop him. She didn't need to explain a hickey to the peahens at work.

He apologized and ventured down her body with his lips, kissing inch by inch down to her belly button. She let out a moan and desired more of what he was giving her. He worked his was further south, inching down the bed and pulled her legs gently apart. He slid off the bed and got down on his knees on the floor and yanked her toward him.

A devilish grin spread across his lips as he leaned in and kissed her sweet spot. He separated her lips with his tongue as he dampened her point of entry. Annaca squirmed as he did this. It tickled but felt amazing. She tried to get him to slow down, but the heat of his breath and the warmth of his tongue slithering in had her eyes rolling into the back of her head.

As her thighs started to tighten around his head, he slid his arms up and pressed her knees into the bed. She groaned as her body started to quiver. Her hands shot up into her hair as she couldn't fight off the oncoming orgasm that quaked through her body.

She moaned with a tremendous "Ohhhh....goodddssss."

With her body shuddering, she encouraged him to come up onto the bed. Her lips quivered as she kissed him gently. She intended to give him the same pleasure in gratitude for the body-shaking experience. She was driven to add her own sensual twist to pleasing him.

He did as she asked and crawled up onto the bed with her and lay down on his back. He clasped his hands behind his head and asked, "What would you like?"

Annaca climbed on top of him and caressed his chest with her hands.

"Well, I am curious as to why you are rushing this." She said as her fingertips traced up around his chest and shoulders.

He didn't say a thing; instead, he pulled her down on top of him and wrapped his arms around her. Her confusion grew, but she welcomed his embrace. She laid her ear against his chest, listening to him breathe. The warmth of his body and the rhythm of his breathing put her to sleep. She was out cold.

When she woke up, she couldn't decide if he had been there or not. When she realized she was still fully clothed and wrapped up in her comforter, she knew. It had only been a dream. She sat up in her bed angrily and thought about it.

Was she in love with him? She winced at the thought. Love is for people who know each other, care for each other and trust one another. It can't be *love*. It has to be *lust*.

She shook her head and got up. Annaca headed to the kitchen when a wave of nausea hit her like a ton of bricks. She put her hand over her mouth and rushed to the bathroom. She sat on the edge of her tub and hovered over the toilet waiting to throw up. Panic flashed through her mind. *Am I sick or am I .... pregnant?*

She was going through a wash of emotions as she hovered over the toilet. Thoughts raced through her mind. *If I am pregnant, it would be Weston's. He was the last person I had sex with, and I had my cycle a week before that took place.*

She couldn't control the spiraling terror that was building up inside of her. Her mouth began to water, and she was about to see her cocoa again.

After an hour of heaving her guts out until she was dry, she cleaned herself up and went back to her bed. She grabbed her phone and called into the office and explained that she had the flu and was going to go to the doctor. Her next phone call was to the receptionist at her doctor's office.

A sweet voice picked up with, "Dr. Main's office, this is Melody, how can I help you today?"

Annaca choked out, "Hey Melody, it's Annaca. I need to see Dr. Main as soon as possible. I think I have the flu again."

Melody replied with, "Oh, you poor thing, okay, I can get you into the office around three today."

"Thank you, Melody. I will see you then." Annaca confirmed.

Annaca hung up the phone and set an alarm for two so she could get up and catch the bus to her doctor's office. She laid back down and tightened the wrap of her comforter around her. She drifted back into a deep, dreamless sleep.

Annaca was startled awake by her alarm. She reached for her phone and tried to silence the alarm. Panic struck her as she remembered why that alarm was set. She jumped out of bed and scrambled around for her purse, door keys, phone and a jacket because she was freezing.

She put her sneakers on and rushed out. She forgot to lock her top door, but she did at least lock the bottom door before she headed to the bus stop. The stop was about half a block from her flat. She tried to run to catch it, in hopes she didn't throw up on her shoes in the process.

Barely making it in time, she reached the stop just as the bus pulled up. A few people climbed onto the bus before her. An elderly woman with a strong perfume had fogged the bus with her scent. Annaca tried to find a seat where she couldn't smell it, but it was no use.

She asked the driver if she could borrow the trash can just in case. Annaca looked sea green, so the driver handed it over immediately. Annaca thanked him and went and sat down with a hand over her nose and mouth and the other clenched to the trash can. The bus started to move on through the stops on its route. Annaca tried to relax as she awaited this doctor's appointment.

The bus finally reached the block that her doctor's office was on, and she couldn't wait to get away from that strongly scented woman. She got to the driver and handed the trash can back and thanked him. She exited the bus and began her walk of misery to the doctor's front door.

The building was quaint and didn't fit into the city at all, but the practice had been there for years. It was a family practice that had been passed down through the generations. They kept it clean and up to date, it was just tiny. Annaca opened the steel door and there sat Melody behind a mound of files and paperwork.

"Hey Melody, did I make it on time?" Annaca inquired.

Melody poked her head around the stack of files and smiled at her.

"Yes, of course. You are right on time. Just sign in here, and the doctor will be with you in a moment."

Annaca scribbled her name in the slot on the clipboard and handed it back to Melody. She looked around for a distracting magazine and sat down.

About twenty minutes had passed when the nurse opened the side door and called for Annaca. Annaca stood up slowly, put down the magazine and followed the nurse into the back. She hung her head because her fate was to be answered soon. Paranoid for the "you're pregnant" statement, she wasn't ready for a child. The nurse directed her to a room about the size of a closet and placed her file on the countertop.

She began to ask her some questions. "So, Ms. Annaca, what brings you into the office today? When was your last menstrual cycle? Any fever, coughing, vomiting?"

Annaca shrugged her shoulders and replied, "I think I either have the flu or I'm pregnant. I have had a fever. I haven't been feeling myself lately, and this morning I threw up until I dry heaved. My last cycle was about four weeks ago. I should be starting anytime, honestly."

The nurse jotted down some notes on her file and asked her to sit on the table. She took her temperature and blood pressure. Next, the nurse asked her to step on the professional scale.

The nurse wrote down her weight, smiled and said, "Alright, Annaca, the doctor will be in with you in a few moments. She is following up with another patient, and then she will see you. I hope you feel better."

The nurse scurried out of the closet and shut the door. Annaca could hear her file slide into the holder on the wall, and then it was silent. Annaca swung her feet back and forth like a little kid as she waited for the doctor. Another fifteen minutes went by, and then the door handle wiggled as the door opened, and Dr. Main walked through.

"Hello Annaca, I see you aren't feeling so hot today. So tell me what's going on. Let's get you back to feeling better."

Annaca drew in a breath and started filling her in on what she was experiencing. "The past three weeks, I really haven't felt well. Today I woke up and basically threw up everything but my shoes. I honestly don't know if it's the flu or that I could be pregnant."

Dr. Main took down some notes as she talked and said, "Alright, well we are going to need a urine sample, and we can do a swab for the flu as well."

Annaca nodded and waited for the nurse to come back in with a sample cup and a cotton swab that would gag anyone. Annaca laid her head down on the cool table and just felt miserable. She hated being sick.

The nurse came back in and said, "Alright, the doctor wants these two samples, and then we can figure out what we need to do."

Annaca nodded and opened her mouth so the nurse could swab her mouth and throat. It was such a horrible feeling. She put the swab back into the package and handed her the urine sample cup.

"You know how this test goes. When you are finished, please place it through the little metal door, then come back to this room and we will have your test results for you shortly. If you need to, you can shut the light off while you wait, just leave the door open and the doctor will be back in with your results."

Annaca nodded and proceeded to walk to the bathroom down the hall.

She knocked and then opened the door. The tile floor made the bathroom sound so empty. Her hand searched for the light and flicked it on. She went through the sample process and placed her little cup into the mini metal two way cabinet. Throwing away the paper towel she used to transport the cup, and then washed her hands.

She glanced in the mirror as she awaited her fate. Turning the light off in the bathroom, she trudged back to the room where she clicked off the light and laid her head down.

Thirty minutes had passed as Annaca was woken up by the doctor. Dr. Main waited for Annaca to sit up and wake herself up enough to talk. The doctor opened the file folder and flicked on the light. She scanned her notes and test results. She looked at Annaca and started off with, "Well my dear, I have some good news and I have some bad news..."

Chapter Eighteen

Moving On

Annaca rubbed her eyes so that she could focus. The florescent-lighting did not help her blurred vision. She stretched and yawned with a body shudder as the doctor flipped through her file. Annaca wanted to get better, but she wasn't ready for bad news.

Doctor Main clicked her pen and wrote down a notation as she started with, "Well, Annaca, we have a couple of options to consider. I do have your test results back, and I have an answer for you."

Annaca leaned back against the cream-colored wall that the cushioned examination table was propped next to. She draped her legs off the side of the table and let her feet dangle and swing back and forth. She was trying to prep herself the best that she could for whatever news the doctor was about to bestow upon her.

"Alright, Doc, just let me have it. I just need to know so I can move forward from this and do whatever I have to do to get better. I'm over being sick and miserable." Annaca sighed.

The doctor nodded in acknowledgement and flipped through the file she was holding in her hands.

Annaca hung her head down as the doctor spoke briskly, "Well, according to your flu swab, you definitely have the flu and your urine test shows positive for pregnancy. Now, I would like to have the nurse draw some blood so we can test for an actual positive. Some urine tests can produce a false positive, so don't panic just yet."

A wave of nausea crashed over Annaca as the thoughts of being pregnant with Weston's child flooded her mind. She wouldn't mind carrying his child, but she was not ready to be a mother.

She stuttered out, "How long will it take to find out for sure?"

The doctor smiled and said, "No worries, my dear. It will only take a couple of hours with our lab. Until then, I'm going to prescribe some low-level antibiotics and nausea medication for you to take. This should help you feel better and be able to keep food down. My nurse will call you with the results as soon as they are in. I suggest that you take the week off to rest up and let the medicine kick in. If you have any other problems or concerns, please call the office."

Annaca sat and waited for the nurse to come back into the room. Maybe a minute had passed by as the nurse pushed the door open with her elbow, carrying a tray with a couple of alcohol swab packets, a syringe, a blue rubber strap and a tube with a heavy-duty burnt orange rubber seal for blood. The nurse set the tray beside Annaca, asked her to pull up her shirtsleeve and make a fist. The nurse grabbed a pair of latex gloves out of a box on the wall and stretched her hands into them.

She tore open an alcohol swab and wiped the crease of Annaca's left arm. Annaca's veins stood out so well that the nurse made a comment about how they were perfect for blood draws. The nurse tied the rubber strap around Annaca's small bicep, and tapped the vein that she was about to stick. She then uncapped the syringe and slowly stuck it into Annaca's pulsating vein.

Annaca winced at the prick but tried to stay calm. The nurse quickly filled the vial and released the strap from Annaca's arm. The nurse then grabbed another swab and placed it over the needle entry point. She gently pulled the needle out and told Annaca to bend her arm to apply pressure. After the nurse finished, she threw the syringe into the sharps container on the wall and asked Annaca if she wanted gauze for her puncture. Annaca shook her head but kept her arm squeezed close.

The nurse smiled and said, "I hope you feel better, sweetie. Get some rest."

Annaca nodded in acknowledgement. She slid off the table and gathered her things. The nurse handed her the file to take to the front desk and check out. Annaca gingerly walked to the front desk.

Melody looked up at Annaca, handed her a note for work and said, "Oh, you poor thing. I hope you feel better. Keep your phone on so we can call you with your test results. Get some rest, sweetie."

Annaca thanked her and headed toward the bus stop. She had to fill her prescriptions, so she walked past her stop and continued to the corner store pharmacy. Feeling utterly miserable, she grabbed a light soda and some crackers and walked down to the drop-off desk of the pharmacy. She leaned against the counter and waited for the pharmacist.

A short woman with a graying sixties-style straight haircut scurried around shelves of medications and supplies as she was trying to fill orders.

The pharmacist held up her hand and hollered from the shelves, "One minute, sweetie, I'm going as fast as I can. My little legs can only move so fast."

Annaca sighed and replied, "Yes, ma'am, take your time. I'm not in a rush, I just need a nap."

A few moments passed, and the pharmacist rushed over to the drop-off desk. "How can I help you today?" She asked.

Annaca looked down with her sleepy eyes and caught the name tag that read, *Cheryl*. "Hi Cheryl, I have a couple of prescriptions that I have to fill." Annaca responded.

Cheryl smiled at her and asked her to give her a few moments. "I'll have these filled up for you, and I can ring up your other items as well."

Annaca sighed and went and sat in the chair until she heard her name called out by Cheryl. Annaca pushed herself up into a standing position and trudged over to the pickup counter, where a register sat. The register looked like an old computer that had yellowed from time. Cheryl rang in Annaca's prescriptions, her drink and crackers.

"Is there anything else I can get for you today?" Cheryl asked.

Annaca shook her head, paid her total and thanked Cheryl. Annaca was ready to curl up in her bed and wait for that last phone call that would decide her future actions.

Annaca finally made it to her little piece of heaven and put everything onto her dining room table. She opened her soda, opened up her medicines and took them with a bubbly swallow. Her bed was calling to her, and she eagerly stumbled to her bed as quickly as her sick body would let her. She greeted Jack and gave him a few pellets of food, plugged her phone in to charge and made sure that the volume was up. She had to know, but until then, she was going to sleep.

Annaca was asleep fast, and her mind was in and out of past sexual encounters. Her body may have been ill, but her mind wanted something else. Visions of Weston danced in her dreams. He was there with her, comforting her. His warm, gentle hands caressed her shoulder and ran down to her elbow. Annaca shifted over so his fingertips would graze closer to her breast that was hidden under a thin camisole.

Weston shook his head and smirked. "You are supposed to be resting."

Annaca smiled and said, "I want more though, how about a quickie to help me sleep?"

Weston leaned in and caressed her lips with his. Annaca returned the kiss eagerly. She rolled over to press her body into his. Weston's muscular arms embraced her body, and his hand slowly washed over her hip and onto her ass. He squeezed her cheek and then smacked it. "Naughty girl, you need to rest."

The sound of the smack didn't sound like a smack, it was a ringing chime. A cell phone was trying to get her attention through chimes and vibrations. Annaca sleepily rolled over and cringed when she saw who was calling her. It was the doctor's office with her future decision.

Annaca picked up the phone and answered with a rough tone in her voice, "Hello?"

The voice on the other end responded with, "Annaca, we have your results. The good news is you are not pregnant. It was a false positive. These things can happen. The doctor sent over a prescription for birth control to your pharmacy that you can pick up anytime. The doctor would also like you to make a follow-up appointment for next week. Would you like to schedule that now or you can call back later."

"I will call you back to schedule. Thank you." Annaca replied.

The voice replied with, "Alright, you have a wonderful day and feel better."

Annaca hung up her phone and groaned as she rolled back over to snuggle into her blankets. She tried to go back to sleep and catch Weston in her dreams, but she was awake and sleep was over.

She sat there and thought about it all. *Well, I don't have to make that phone call, but I don't think it would have mattered. He probably wouldn't respond,* anyway.

She felt anger rise in her at the thought of him being so elusive. She hated that he never answered unless he wanted something, and it pained her. This man was breaking her heart, and she was livid. Her mind and body desired him, yet her heart wanted to punch him in the face for never responding to any type of message.

More than anything, she was frustrated with herself for letting her emotions get involved. She knew better than to get her hopes up with a man. *They say we are the crazy ones who don't know what we want, yet, I don't think they know what they want either.* She thought.

Although she did tell him that she wasn't expecting any-thing, he kept leading her on with the invite to the farm and the random hookups. It was her fault, though. She started this thing with Weston; she went after him. She could have left him alone and never followed him.

She sat up in her bed and decided to take a break from the social world. She would work and spend time catching up on her favorite books and her fish. Maybe she would get him a friend. No point in them both being lonely. She wanted to reset her mind and give her heart a chance to heal. This pain would only turn her feelings off, but she needed the time to decide what she wanted to do with her life.

She refused to sit around and wait on a man who asked her to the farm, but didn't bother to follow up with an address or a "Hey, I'm on my way to get you."

Annaca wanted something more, a partner maybe, that would keep up with her sexual appetite, but would also enjoy the peace of down time along with the occasional fun of exploring. So far, everyone she has met hasn't fulfilled her expectations in a partner. They have only filled her with more lustful intentions.

Note to my Readers

(November 4, 2025)

The false positive did actually happen to me, even though I do in fact have 4 very healthy children. My oldest (now 25) has given me two beautiful grandchildren, and now we are expecting another in Sept. 2025.

I do apologize if the situation does bother people, but it is a part of life and it does happen. Plus, if I put a trigger warning about it before the story, it would ruin the ending.

Your mental health does matter to me, and I hope you enjoy my future books.

About the Author

K. B. Rebel (Kat Jackson) is a stay at home mom of a child with Down syndrome along with three other children. She is a retired DJ of 27 years and now writes during the day as an independent author. She is a chicken tender for many feathered babies and a caregiver of many other animals. Her dream is to share her stories with others. Not all of her stories are smut. She has a few other books in the works and doesn't plan to stop writing ever.

Contact the Author:

Email: authorkbrebel@gmail.com

Facebook: KBRebelAuthor

Tiktok: @author_k.b.rebel

Instagram: @author_k.b.rebel

Threads: @author_k.b.rebel

Also by K. B. Rebel (Kat Jackson)

Lustful Ventures (Book Two, April 2025)

Lustful Endeavors (Book Three, August 2025)

Triple Awakening: Origin (April 2025)

Triple Awakening: Fury (2026)

Devious Whispers (2026)

Dedication

Thank you for taking the time to read a debut novel by an independent author. The first chapter of this book sat for exactly one year before I decided to work on chapters two and three. My daughter, Savannah, was my inspiration to write. She would always try to encourage me to put a book together. The origin of this particular book began with my appetite for romance novels. Normally, this isn't material to dedicate to anyone, but the fact that I was encouraged to write is why I thank those around me.

The first person I started to badger was my sister, Cynthia. I love her more than she will ever know. She gave me the hope that I needed to work and write. I will always be grateful for everything she has ever done for me, and she better know it.

My two best friends have had to deal with me being a pest and my anxiety as I have tried to create this book. They have been encouraging and proud of me from the start. Bryan and Jared are the most amazing friends a girl could ever ask for. Someday I hope to marry them off to some amazing women who will know that I am only a text message away. I think that they deserve the world for having to deal with my craziness. I love you guys, and I look forward to many more nights of driving you crazy about chapters.

A funny story is that while I was an active DJ and Karaoke hostess, I was also working on my book in the DJ booth. One, typical Saturday night in June, I met a wallflower that just happened to be in my bar for the first time. Ironically, we had met before through a dating app. We clicked again quickly. When I gave him my number, I wrote it on the back of a blue index card that I had been doodling a flower on, and I told him to text me because I hated being on the phone.

He read a draft of my book on a road trip, which made it an awkward trip. We talked about everything before we decided to officially date. The funny part about this, he came over to my house after work one day to show me his F150 and on the front of the truck was the word *Westin*. I had no clue because I hadn't known him until after I had written my first draft. Needless to say, we were married on Halloween of 2020. (What a crazy year). We have been inseparable since that fateful day he walked into my bar.

Last but most important of all, my mom, Merry. She has worked hard with me to help edit and add her *Grammar Nazi* touch to all that I have written. I am thankful for the life that she has given me, the support to be whatever I wanted and all the love. I took a four-year break after first publishing this novel thanks to the troubles of life. Losing my mother to lung cancer in 2024 was my kick in the ass to get back to work and refine this book. Now, I am writing almost every day. I miss her more than I can ever write about.

Bottom line, my inspiration has come from many sources and influences. Along with large quantities of imagination and with a few personal experiences. Stay tuned for future books and happy reading!

~Always K.B. Rebel (Kat)~